Tales from the Canyons of the Damned

DANIEL ARTHUR SMITH

Tales from the Canyons of the Damned No. 14

First Edition

Special thanks to Jessica West

ISBN-13: 978-1946777218 ISBN-10: 1946777218

Cover By Daniel Arthur Smith

Horror Fiction from Holt Smith ltd
Agroland
Tower

~*~

For Susan, Tristan, & Oliver, as all things are.

~*~

Pod Fifteen

Philip Harris

~*~

Ellis stared at the face of the dead man and tried to guess his name. "How about Danny?"

Incorrect.

"Really? He looks like a Danny to me. Or a Pete. Either Pete or Sid."

Both Pete and Sid are incorrect.

"All right, I give in."

The subject's name was Marcus Wilson.

"Okay, a Marcus. That sounds like a salesman's name. Probably sold real estate or something."

Marcus Wilson was a motivation speaker for the Trigenics Corporation.

"See? He was selling people a better life. One point to me. How many does that make now?"

You have earned three points since leaving Denia.

"That's a record."

Correct.

"Right, now for the important bit." Ellis ran his fingers through his greasy hair. He couldn't remember when he'd last showered. "He looks pretty pale, even for a dead guy. Probably died due to loss of blood somehow. He get stabbed by an irate customer?"

Incorrect.

"Hit by a car?"

Incorrect.

"Suicide."

Incorrect.

Ellis sighed. "Okay, how did this one bite the dust?"

Marcus Wilson was killed in a skiing accident. Primary cause of death was epidural hematoma.

Ellis winced. "Ouch."

He considered kicking off another round of the game, but he was tired and his hands were shaking slightly. He switched off the display.

"Lisa, confirm travel time."

It has been three weeks, six hours, fifty-two minutes, and seventeen seconds since we left the station.

"Three weeks, huh? In that case, I think it must be time to switch up your vocal settings. Let's try female this time. Just pick something at random and give me a test phrase."

Understood.

Welcome aboard the Deep Space Transport Vessel Redhawk, Pilot Osako.

Ellis winced. "No, I don't think so. That sounds too much like my ex-wife. Try something a bit more girl next door."

I do not understand, girl next door.

"You know: nice, polite, intelligent. The sort of girl my mom would have wanted me to marry."

A pause.

Welcome aboard the Deep Space Transport Vessel Redhawk, Pilot Osako.

Ellis smiled. "That's more like it. Accept."

Vocal Option Three Eighty-four selected.

The console in front of Ellis let out a low buzz. A red light flickered on for a few seconds, then went dark again.

"Lisa, run a diagnostics sweep. Let's make sure this pile of junk is going to get us where we're going."

Beginning internal diagnostics.

"Thank you. I'll be in my executive suite. Don't wake me unless the ship catches fire."

Understood.

Ellis climbed out of the pilot's chair, opened the door to his quarters, and walked inside. The door juddered almost closed behind him. He kicked the lower corner and it lurched the final couple of inches. The room was just over twenty feet long and half as wide, just enough room for a bunk and a small metal locker that served as his closet, pantry and bookshelf. A second door, this one barely wide enough to qualify as one, led into the bathroom with its shower and fold out sink. It was one of the few things on the Redhawk that could actually be considered a luxury.

An almost empty bottle of bourbon stood on the floor beside the narrow strip of foam that served as his mattress. The foam sat on top of a sheet of metal welded to the outer hull. When he tried to sleep, he could feel the vibration of the ship's engines. He grabbed the bottle and shook it, then sighed and sat down. Three weeks in and he was down to the last quarter of the bourbon. At least he had other, more inventive ways to numb the tedium.

He lay back on the bed, the bourbon clutched to his chest like a teddy bear. The last pilot had taped a poster of some model Ellis didn't recognize to the ceiling. Its ink had faded until the man's pale blue eyes were almost completely white, and a corner curled up where one of the tacks had come free. Ellis had found the tack in his bed half way through his first night, but not bothered to push it back in.

The hull beside his head groaned. He still wasn't used to the sound. No, scratch that. He was used to it, he was just convinced it was a sign that the Redhawk was going to disintegrate before they reached Kiran. If that happened, he wondered whether the Denians would dispatch some sort of cleanup crew to pick up the ship's cargo and take it on to their beloved burial planet. And if they did, would they take his body along as well? Just for good measure?

He pinched the bridge of his nose. A familiar high-pitched whine was just creeping into his consciousness. In half an hour, it would settle in at the edge of his hearing—just too loud for him to ignore. There it would sit, gradually driving him insane until he grabbed the nearest sharp implement and jammed it into his brains to scratch that infuriating, tinnitus-derived itch.

Unless he took his medicine.

He held up the bottle of bourbon. Alcohol had long since stopped having any real effect on him. There just wasn't enough weight allowance on a long-haul job to bring enough to manage anything beyond a mild buzz. He'd brought the bourbon out of a misplaced sense of nostalgia rather than anything else.

The tinnitus grew stronger, drowning out the distant rumble of the Redhawk's engines for a few seconds before fading away again. It would be back.

Ellis sat up on the edge of the bunk and opened the locker door. If he'd needed to, he could reach the back of it from where he was sitting, but he kept his medicine close at hand. He stood the bourbon on the floor, just inside the locker, and pulled a wooden box from a shelf.

The box's surface was scratched and worn, and the smell of the cigars it had once held was almost gone, but he only really cared about what was inside it. He flipped the lid and smiled when he saw the familiar envelopes— tiny squares barely bigger than his thumbnail. They were made of paper so thin you could see the shadows of their contents if you held them up to the light. The front of each one was painted with an intricate, abstract pattern that told connoisseurs like Ellis the exact pedigree of the medicine they were handling. They were works of art, really.

He flicked through the envelopes, looking for the blue stamp of his favorite brand. If he'd had the money, he'd have stocked up on more but he'd get through a lot of medicine in three and a half months. The Trisense Corporation weren't paying him that well.

The little stack of what he liked to call *Epic Blue* was at the back of the box—five envelopes. That meant half of it was gone already. He opened his mouth and twisted his jaw from side to side in an effort to dislodge the growing tinnitus. As always, it didn't help.

He removed one of the *Epic Blue* envelopes and placed the box back on the shelf. Sitting back on the bunk, he wiped the palm of his left hand on the rough blanket. Satisfied there was no moisture on it, he carefully squeezed the sides of the envelope until it popped open. Then he tipped the circle of medicine out onto his palm. He knew better than to savor this part of the ritual—he'd ruined more than one dose by letting it stick to his hand. He lifted the paper-thin disk to his mouth and lapped it up like a dog.

Closing his eyes, he lay back on the bunk. Heat spread across his tongue. Its progress slowed, and, for a moment, he was afraid he'd been ripped off and it was a bad batch. Then the warmth crept up the inside of his cheeks and across the roof of his mouth. Tendrils of pleasure wormed their way through his body, chasing away the darkness with their light. His heart stuttered and there was the usual instant of panic where his body instinctively feared for its survival. Then his heart resumed its steady beat and his thoughts lit up like fireworks.

~*~

"Good morning, Lisa."

Good morning, Pilot.

"Diagnostics show up anything interesting?"

The ship is operating at ninety-three point two percent efficiency. All systems are within acceptable limits. Engine capacity is at seventy-eight percent.

"Good, good."

Ellis brushed his hand across the thick stubble on his chin. The tinnitus had gone for now, and he actually found himself smiling. He jumped into the pilot's seat and pushed off with his feet. The articulated arm that connected the seat to the ceiling carried him across the bridge to main console and its display screen.

"Bring up the crypt."

The screen flickered to life and revealed the ship's cargo hold.

"Lights."

Two dozen LED lights burst to life, revealing a series of rectangular metal pods laid out in neat rows. Each pod had three large white digits painted on it. There were one hundred and eighty of them in total—the precious, lifeless cargo Ellis was responsible for getting to Kiran in one piece.

Ellis swept his finger over the screen. "Eeny, meeny, miny... mo!" He jabbed his finger down. "I'll take corpse number fifty-seven for three points."

The display changed to a close up of a man's face, dark skinned and deeply lined. He was bald, and the puckered edge of a scar curved around the front of his skull.

"Hm, he looks like a Richard."

Incorrect.

"Are you sure?"

Yes.

"Leroy?"

Incorrect.

"Derek?"

Incorrect. The subject's name is Nathan Meadows.

"He died of a brain tumor or something though, right?"

Correct. A glioblastoma multiforme.

"How old was he? Sixty-three?"

At time of death, he was approximately seventy-one years old.

"Wow, he looks pretty good for his age. Apart from the whole operating scar thing."

Lisa didn't reply.

"Okay, show me the crypt again."

The display changed back to the rows of metal boxes. The white numbers glowed under the harsh lights.

Ellis studied the screen. "Let's go with number fifteen."

A young Asian woman's face appeared on the screen.

Ellis stared at the image for several long seconds before he spoke. "Her name was Lucy. She was nineteen when she died, a student. She'd just started at college and had gone to a drugstore to stock up on some basics—

milk, bread." Ellis took a deep breath. "Some punk-ass kid came in waving a gun around. The owner pulled a shotgun out and tried to shoot the kid. He missed and hit Lucy. She died in the hospital later that night. Alone."

There was a pause.

Incorrect.

Ellis pushed the pilot's chair back to the main control panel. "Turn it off."

As the display died, Ellis stood. Without speaking, he walked slowly into his quarters.

~*~

Ellis sat in the cargo hold, opposite pod fifteen. He'd never seen inside any of the pods, but from the outside, they looked more like ordinary containers that might carry a shipment of food or electronics. They were just long, rectangular boxes. Each one had a small panel on the outside with a keypad and a single LED that shone green to show the pod's seal was intact.

He stared at the rectangular identification plate riveted to the side of the pod. There was a picture of the woman on it—the kind of bland image that government organizations demanded be captured for passports and driving licenses. Despite the banality of the photograph, there was a noticeable brightness in her eyes—some spark within her hiding just beneath the surface, ready to break out and show itself when the serious photographic business was done.

The panel gave her name too: Tenshi Kuro. She'd been twenty-four when she died. There was other information—her weight, height, place of birth—but Ellis was drawn to the photograph. He stared at it, afraid to blink, until his eyes began to water.

The bottle of bourbon was sitting on the floor between his legs. He picked it up and took a mouthful, his eyes not leaving the image of the woman in the coffin even as the liquor burned his throat. The bourbon sloshed loudly as he placed it back on the floor. The bottle was almost empty.

Out of the corner of his eye, he saw the LED on the container flicker. His eyes darted to it. He was convinced it had changed color, but it still shone green. The pod was sealed. He felt a pang of disappointment, and, for a few seconds, considered opening it himself. There was a protocol for gaining access to a pod, although he had no idea on what grounds it might be justified. Certainly, he had no reason to disturb the woman's body.

He took another drink, savoring the alcohol's heat and letting it burn away the urge to open the pod. No good could come of that. Tears formed at the corners of his eyes and he tried to convince himself it was just the drink.

"Lisa, run a diagnostics check on pod fifteen, please."

There was a brief pause.

All systems operating within expected ranges. Hermetic seal intact.

Another pause.

As was the case when you made your third enquiry, seventeen minutes ago.

Ellis wiped the back of his hand across his mouth and sniffed. His fingers were trembling. He held his hand up to his face and stared at his fingers, willing them to still. His index finger twitched as if in rebellion. He let his hand drop again.

His fingers sought out the label on the bottle resting between his legs and started peeling it away. His wife had told him once that peeling labels from bottles was a sign of sexual frustration. He smiled sadly at the memory of the passionate rebuttal that had followed. That had been before fate had torn them apart. He squeezed his eyes shut for a few seconds, trying to dislodge the memory. Then he ripped off another scrap of label, rolled it into a ball and flicked it away. It rebounded off the side of the pod and fell through a gap in the floor.

"I'm sorry." The words came out fragmented. Tears welled in his eyes again. "I'm sorry, Lucy."

Ellis drained the last of the bourbon. A sudden burst of anger hit him, and he sent the bottle flying across the room. It hit the wall and shattered. Shards of glass rained down onto the floor like ice crystals. He let his head drop forward and pressed his hands against his face. They smelled of bourbon and sweat. He sobbed.

He ran his hands down his face and licked his lips. His mouth was gummy, thick with dense saliva. He clenched his hands until his knuckles turned white, then opened them and watched his fingers twitch and shake. Some unseen piece of the ship's mechanisms clunked somewhere beneath the floor. He slid over to the pod and knelt beside it. The LED glowed green. He ran his fingertips lightly over the keypad.

"Lisa, give me the access code for pod fifteen."

Trisense procedures state that access to cargo pods by contracted employees is prohibited.

"Unless there's an emergency."

I do not detect an emergency situation.

"No, I suppose you don't." Ellis sighed. "Just give me the code."

Trisense procedures state that access to cargo containers by contracted employees is prohibited. The consequences for unauthorized access include termination of employment and substantial fines.

"I'm overriding the procedure. I'll deal with the consequences."

Understood. Access code 90410756.

Ellis tapped the first seven digits into the keypad. His index finger rested on the final key. He held it there, willing the withdrawal to take the decision away from him, but his finger held steady. He tapped the CANCEL button, and the control panel gave a disgruntled beep.

He ran his fingers over the identification plate, tracing the woman's image. Then he turned and leaned his back against the pod. He tipped his head up and stared into the harsh light above until his eyes began to water and he was forced to look away. Patches of light danced across his vision when he blinked.

"I'm sorry."

He reached into his pocket and pulled out a tiny envelope of *Epic Blue*. His hands shook as he squeezed the edges of the packet and tipped the disk of medicine out onto his palm.

There was no tinnitus yet, but he could feel it circling, biding its time. It would be back before long. He raised his hand and dabbed his tongue against the disk.

The familiar warming sensation spread across his tongue and along the roof of his mouth. He held his breath, waiting for the drug to reach his heart. Even then, when the lurching, hesitant beats came, he felt the same grasping fear he always did. His heart seemed to take an age to settle and enough time passed that he began to wonder if he'd finally pushed his aging body too far. When it finally calmed down, he closed his eyes and let his head fall back against the pod as the drug worked its magic.

~*~

Three hours later, Ellis carefully made his way to the bridge. The medicine lingered at the back of his mind, and, for the moment, the sharp edges of his memories had been worn smooth. Smooth enough for him to function, anyway. If he concentrated hard enough, he could conjure up the last vestiges of its effects—a gentle tickling of his pleasure sensors and the warm glow of a life well lived.

It took three attempts to get the door to the bridge to open. When it finally did, it let out a grinding, metallic complaint and only opened eighty percent of the way.

"This ship is falling apart."

Sensors indicate all systems are operating within expected parameters.

"Yeah? Well, Trisense need to adjust their parameters. I'm going to write them a stern letter when we get to Kiran."

I would suggest an electronic form of communication. Routing of physical items is often unreliable.

"Okay, I'll send them an email. Whatever, this rust bucket is past its retirement age." Ellis held up a hand. "Don't bother replying to that. It's just a figure of speech."

Understood.

Ellis climbed into the pilot's chair and kicked off so that it swung around the cabin before returning to the main console. "Start a short-range scan." He paused. "No, wait. We'll do that later." He tapped his fingers against the edge of the console. "Bring up the record for Tenshi Kuro."

The main display changed to the image of the woman in pod fifteen.

"Give me split screen. Put her photograph on segment one."

The display flickered. Her image appeared on the left-hand side. Ellis considered it for a moment before he spoke again. "Access my personal files. Play file *Xmas39* on segment two."

The right side of the display turned black for a few seconds, then a video appeared. It showed an Asian girl of four or five riding a red bicycle along a pathway in a garden. A glittering silver bow was stuck to the handlebars. The bike wavered unsteadily as the girl struggled to keep it upright, but her face was filled with joy. A woman followed along behind, her hands ready to catch the girl if she fell.

The girl squeezed the brakes, and the bike rolled to a halt. It tipped sideways and almost fell, but the girl managed to catch it. Once the bike was under control, she looked up at the camera and waved. The woman behind the girl clapped her hands and grinned, almost as excited as the girl herself.

There was a cut, and the video changed to show the girl riding away from the camera. The woman was standing beside the path, still smiling. The camera tilted down and then the video restarted.

"Play file *Sept54*."

The video of the girl on the bike was replaced by a shot of a car laden down with boxes. A young woman was pushing a sleeping bag into the car's trunk, crushing it between two bulging suitcases.

"Bring up the sound."

A man's laughter came from somewhere near the camera. "Are you sure you're taking enough stuff, Lucy?"

The woman from the first video, older now, came into view. "Leave her alone."

"Yeah, dad," said Lucy, "leave me alone. It's my comfort blanket."

"I know, and those are your two dozen comfort dresses, your comfort makeup kit, and your comfort pots and pans."

Lucy tilted her head and stuck her tongue out at the camera.

The video cut to another angle, showing Lucy standing beside the car.

The older woman walked into view. "Are you sure you don't want to take some food? We've got plenty."

"We have comfort milk," said the male voice.

Lucy rolled her eyes. "No, I'll pick some up when I get there."

"Well, if you're su—"

"I'm sure. I need to get going."

The older woman sighed and held her arms wide. Lucy stepped into them and they hugged.

"We could come with you," said the woman.

"No, I'll be fine."

"All right, well, you take care, honey."

"I will, mom. I promise."

The woman sighed and blinked away tears, then released her grip.

Lucy stepped back and swung open the driver's door.

A cough came from behind the camera. "Aren't you forgetting something?"

Lucy frowned and looked up into the sky, her finger pressed against her chin as though she was deep in thought. "No, I don't think so…"

"Lucy…"

Lucy grinned. "Oh yeah, the old man wants a hug too." She turned and held her arms out.

The video cut again. Lucy was sitting in the driver's seat and the engine was running.

"I'm going to miss her," said the older woman.

"Me too," said the man, "but we'll see her again next weekend."

Lucy turned and waved at the camera.

"Pause and zoom in," said Ellis.

The image on the screen froze and then slowly zoomed in on Lucy until her face filled the right-hand side of the screen.

Ellis stared at the faces of the two women on the screen, the warmth of the medicine's effects replaced by a deep, aching loss.

A buzzing came from the control panel beneath the screen and an LED turned red.

Ellis tapped it. The light stayed on. "Are you seeing any—"

Warning. Collision imminent.

He barely had time to grab the edge of the console before a heavy grinding sound ripped through the belly of the ship. He was thrown sideways, the movement almost hurling him out of his seat. The shriek of tearing metal reverberated through the bridge. A red light above the door to his cabin strobed. There was the hiss of pressurized air being vented. A siren started up, pulsing in time to the flashing light.

"Status report!"

Diagnostics scan in progress. Initial readings indicate a collision with debris of indeterminate origin and composition. Localized structural damage. Self-repair systems have been deployed.

"Localized to where?"

Sensors suggest extensive damage to the midship computing center. Additional damage to forward hull.

A low-pitched metallic groan echoed beneath Ellis' feet. The floor shuddered. A bank of lights on the control panel changed from green to red.

"Any more debris out there?"

There was a pause. More hissing came from the direction of his quarters. The red lights turned green again.

Unknown. Damage to internal and external sensor arrays has resulted in minimal environment scanning ability.

Ellis tapped the screen on the control panel. A map of the ship appeared. Three patches of red marred the outer edge—two along the right-hand side near the main computer systems, the third on the front right corner. That one was a direct hit on his cabin.

"Dammit! Okay, full stop."

Initiating deceleration sequence.

"What's the status of my cabin?"

A significant pressure drop has been detected.

"Which means what exactly?"

There is a high likelihood of interior damage.

"Is the locker intact?"

Unknown. Internal sensors currently operating at three percent.

"Any danger to the rest of the ship?"

Unknown. Internal sensors currently operating at three percent.

"Okay, the ship's broken. I get it. Turn that damn siren off!"

The siren cut out, revealing the dull throb of the engines as they slowed the ship.

Ellis looked toward the red flashing light above the cabin door. Each pulse hammered a tiny icepick into the center of his skull, between his eyes. "And the light."

The light flashed twice more, then stopped.

Ellis tapped his hand against his thigh. His right foot bounced up and down on the chair's footrest. After a few seconds, he stood and went over to the cabin. "Okay, let me take a look." He tapped the control panel beside the door.

Access to the pilot's quarters is not permitted. Internal pressure within the cabin is now at eight percent of expected range.

"And opening the door would depressurize the bridge?"

Correct.

"Any damage in the crypt? Wait, don't tell me. Unknown."

Correct. Internal sensors—

"Yeah, yeah. I understood the first time." He pointed to the bank of lights on the console that had turned red. "What do those lights mean? Bank 4A."

Bank 4A denotes the sensor array within the cargo hold.

"Those lights turned red just after the impact. Why?"

Unknown.

"Bring up the cargo hold camera."

The display flickered, but instead of showing the pods, the screen turned to a solid block of magenta.

"The camera's down?"

Correct.

Ellis pressed his fingers against the point where the ice pick had entered his skull. "Of course it is." He shook his head. "Can you at least tell me whether I can make a manual inspection?"

Damage appears to be limited to exterior and directly adjacent areas. At this time, there is no indication of a hull breach in the cargo hold or the main corridor.

The rumble of the engines faded, leaving behind a hollow silence.

Ship velocity now zero.

"Any estimate on how long before the systems are back up?"

Current estimate is twenty-seven hours, forty minutes. Margin of error plus/minus thirty-seven percent.

Ellis let his head drop down onto the control panel. It landed with a dull thump that did nothing to shift the pain within. The familiar whine of the tinnitus rose into his consciousness. Groaning, he raised his head and looked toward his cabin. The light above the door was still red. He gritted his teeth, then sighed. "I'm going to check the crypt. Let me know if any of those unknowns become knowns."

Yes, Pilot Osako.

"And get that breach in my cabin fixed."

Yes, Pilot Osako.

~*~

The cargo hold took up the bulk of the ship. Apart from the bridge and the tiny living quarters, there was a just a narrow corridor that led to a solitary airlock and the hold itself. There weren't even any lifeboats. In the event of an emergency, the bridge and cabin module could be detached, but it had no engines. If anything major went wrong, he'd probably be better off strapping himself into one of the pods. At least they were guaranteed to be airtight, and he suspected Trisense considered them more valuable than the ship's lone pilot.

Ellis stopped off at the airlock and climbed into one of the lightweight EVA suits. He carried the helmet down the corridor to the entrance to the hold.

The lights on the door panel were green, indicating the cargo hold was safe. Given the state of the ship's systems, he didn't exactly trust the lights. He pulled on the helmet and flicked a switch on the chest plate. There was a hiss, and the helmet filled with oxygen. The helmet silenced the creaks and groans of the ship and seemed to amplify the tinnitus to a level that was almost impossible to ignore. He tapped the *open door* icon. A metal grinding sound came from somewhere inside the wall and the door shuddered open.

Most of the LED strips in the ceiling were still working. One bank, on the left-hand side, had failed creating a dark patch over a few of the pods. He could see why the camera wasn't working. It hung askew on its mount. The green light on the top should have been blinking, but it had gone out. He walked over to left-hand side of the room, beneath the camera. The mounting bracket was twisted, and one of the bolts that held it in place was lying on the floor. He picked it up, rolling it in his fingers. It felt icy cold.

Ellis slipped the bolt into his jacket pocket. The patch of darkness was at the other end of the room. He stared at it. His breath sounded harsh inside the helmet. A growing sense of unease made him turn away and walk across to the opposite side of the room.

He made his way up and down the rows, stopping at each pod. The LEDs were all green, but Ellis crouched and ran his fingers around the edges of each one to check the seal anyway. He'd already discovered three of his 'passengers' had died of particularly virulent contagions. Protocols were in place to make sure any infections were neutralized, but he had no intention of testing the efficacy of that process.

The patch of darkness seemed to hang at the corner of his vision. He made a point of not looking at it, and when he got to the start of the last row, he almost decided to assume the rest of the pods were intact and head back to the bridge.

"Lisa, how are those repairs coming?"

Internal sensors are now operating at eleven percent efficiency. Preliminary self-repairs are underway. Current estimate for a return to full operating capacity is twenty-nine hours, seven minutes. Margin of error plus/minus twenty-three percent.

"So, the estimate went up, but now you're more confident it's right?"

Correct.

The tinnitus grew stronger for a few seconds, then died back down to a volume that was slightly above its previous level.

"Anything we can do to speed up the repairs? Redirect some power from the toilet or something?"

Negative. The energy requirements of the waste disposal system are dependent on usage patterns.

"What if I hold it in? Never mind."

Ellis let out a slow breath. The helmet redirected some of it across his face, and he caught the bitter tang of a mouth that hadn't seen toothpaste for several days.

His knees cracked as he couched beside the next pod. Ignoring the bright green LED, he ran his fingers along the edge of the container. The seal was intact. He thumped the side of the lid for good measure, then moved on to the next one.

As he approached the patch of blackness, he kept his eyes lowered and focused on the pods. Without really knowing why, his inspections became slower and more careful the closer he got to the broken lighting.

There were three containers in the dark area. Some of the light from the LED banks on either side spilled over them, but the rest were swallowed up as though a cloud of some invisible light absorbing material hung above those particular pods.

The LED on the first container, number sixteen, shone clearly in the gloom. He briefly considered trusting the sensors this time, just to get things over with, then forced himself to kneel and check the seal. It was still intact.

He stood and moved on to number fifteen, knowing what he'd find. The LED would be red, and the container's lid would be knocked aside to reveal Tenshi's rotting corpse.

The LED was green. His hands shook as he ran them around the edge of the container, whether from stress or lack of medicine, he couldn't be sure. He checked the seal twice, then shoved the lid, trying to dislodge it. The pod remained intact.

Ellis let out a slow breath as he stood. As soon as he moved past pod fifteen, his uneasiness began to fade. The LED on fourteen was green, too, and when he checked the seal, it was undamaged.

The remaining pods stretched out in front of him. Each one was marked by a green LED. Now he was out of the dark patch, Ellis moved quickly again. He checked the seal on each container carefully but with no real expectation that it would be broken.

When he got to the end of the row, he unclipped his helmet and raised it a couple of inches. The air in the hold had a burned edge to it, but seemed breathable. He removed the helmet and clipped it to his belt.

"Lisa, it seems like the crypt is pretty much intact. The camera took a hit somehow and one of the LED banks is down, but the pods are still sealed. You can reduce the priority of repairs to this section of the ship. These guys won't care."

Understood.

Ellis rubbed his temples. A dull throbbing, fueled by the whining in his ears, had taken up residence deep inside his skull. Time for some medicine. He walked back toward the entrance to the hold. The LED on fifteen was still green. As he reached the door, he turned back. The room seemed less oppressive now. Even the patch of darkness seemed brighter.

He tapped the door control. There was a low-pitched buzz and the LED on the panel turned red. Frowning,

Ellis tapped the screen again. Another buzz. The sound seemed to exacerbate the ringing in his ears.

"Lisa, I need you to unlock the door to the crypt. The panel's not working."

The tinnitus rose on a wave, drowning out the computer's reply. The LED remained red.

"Lisa, open the cargo hold door."

If there was a reply, the ringing in his ears swallowed it up completely.

A spike of pain jammed itself into Ellis' forehead. He cried out, grabbing his head and dropping to his knees. "Lisa!" The door in front of him stayed resolutely closed.

Waves of pain washed over him. Blood dripped from his nose and splashed against the gray metal floor. The world swam. The ringing in his ears ebbed and flowed, coming back stronger with each passing wave. Ellis crushed his hands against his ears. He fell onto his side. The lights seemed to flicker, and then darkness overwhelmed him.

~*~

Cold.

Ice pressed against Ellis' cheek.

Slowly, he opened his eyes.

A face swam in front of him. The pressure on his cheek disappeared. He blinked, dragging the face into focus. The woman from pod fifteen, Tenshi Kuro, stared down at him.

Adrenaline flooded his system, setting his heart racing and sending cold fingers of dread down his spine. He kicked out, pushing himself away from the woman until his back slammed hard against the reassuring metal of the door. "What are you doing? How…"

Tenshi took a step back. She was wearing a white jumpsuit that crackled like plastic as she moved. There was fear in her eyes. She glanced nervously left and right as though searching for a way out. At the other end of the cargo hold, the bank of LED lights were still out but Ellis could see the silhouette of pod fifteen was different to the rest. The lid had been removed.

He looked back at Tenshi, holding her wide-eyed gaze. Looking at her set his heart aching. "I-I'm sorry. You caught me off guard. You don't need to be afraid."

Tenshi frowned, and Ellis realized he wasn't even sure that she could understand him. He knew a little bit of Denian, but only enough to get the medicine he needed. He held up his hands, palms toward her. She flinched a little.

"Can you understand me?"

The woman nodded, hesitantly.

"Okay, good. That's good. You're Tenshi, right?"

She opened her mouth as if to speak but the only sound that came out was a harsh whisper. She tried again, and this time managed to form the word.

"Y-yes."

Ellis felt a twinge of disappointment. He'd known the woman's name but part of him had hoped for a different answer.

He smiled. There were so many questions. Where should he start? Where *could* he start? Tenshi smiled hesitantly back at him, and the ache in his heart deepened.

"I'm going to stand up, okay?"

Tenshi took a half step backward, but nodded.

Trying not to move too quickly, Ellis got to his feet. He smiled again. "Are you hurt?"

Tenshi shook her head. There were dark smudges under her eyes, and her white jumpsuit only served to accentuate her pale complexion.

"Good. Are you tired? Do you need some rest?" Ellis almost slapped his forehead the moment the words were out. "No, of course not."

Tenshi glanced over her shoulder, toward the pods.

"We need to go." Her voice was a whisper, but he could sense the fear beneath it.

"Sure, okay. I just need to…" He hesitated, trying to work out how to explain Lisa. "I'm going to talk to someone else so don't be surprised if you hear another voice, okay?"

Tenshi nodded.

"Lisa, can you get the door to the cryp— to the cargo hold open?"

The door slid open, but Lisa didn't reply.

"Lisa?"

Yes, Pilot Osako.

Ellis felt a sudden surge of unexpected relief at hearing the computer's voice. He glanced at Tenshi. "I'm coming back to the bridge. We have company."

Understood.

He moved to one side and directed Tenshi toward the door. She peered through as though she was expecting an ambush. When none presented itself, she walked through the door, keeping as far away from Ellis as she could.

He let her get a few feet down the corridor before following her. The door slid smoothly shut behind him. There was a soft click as the locking mechanism latched.

With the door closed, Tenshi's mood seemed to change. The fear had gone, replaced by a look of intense sorrow. "I'm sorry."

Puzzled, Ellis frowned. "Why? What have you got to be sorry about?"

"I can't protect you."

"From what? We're the only people on the ship."

Tenshi looked toward the cargo hold door. The fear returned to her face, just for an instant. She smiled at him, but it looked forced.

"Come on," Ellis said, "let's get you warmed up."

They were halfway to the bridge when he realized the throbbing in his skull and the tinnitus were gone.

Tenshi followed Ellis onto the bridge. When she saw her own image on the main display, she frowned.

Ellis saw the look on her face and hurried to turn off the display. "Yeah, um, I was just… passing the time."

Tenshi looked at him and gave him a half smile. She crossed her arms and rubbed her shoulders.

Ellis ran his fingers through his hair. "You look cold."

She nodded.

"There's a shower, if you'd like one. The water's pretty hot."

"Thank you."

Ellis took a step toward the door to his quarters, then remembered the collision.

"Lisa, how are those repairs to my suite going?"

Hull integrity has been restored. Air pressure and composition are normal.

"Great."

He tapped the control panel. The door slid smoothly open to reveal the aftermath of explosive decompression. The foam on the bunk was almost completely gone—the only piece that had survived was a chunk snagged on a twisted fragment of metal. The locker had been torn from the wall. Its battered remains lay beside the metal bunk. The shredded corner of a jacket peaked out from beneath the locker. Chunks of broken mirror were strewn across the cabin. The poster that had been tacked to the wall was gone.

Attached to the wall about two feet above the bunk there was a ragged patch of metal. Thick welding, the precise, almost perfect work of the ship's self-repair units, ran around its edge. Beside the patch, a triangular piece of metal was embedded in the wall. It was another piece of the locker.

"What happened?" Tenshi said.

Ellis started. "Oh, we hit something, and it punctured the hull."

"This was yours?"

He nodded.

"I'm sorry."

Ellis tried to shrug off the damage, but his eyes kept being drawn back to the locker. Pulling them away, he opened the door to the bathroom. "Shower's in there. Green button to start it. Give it a few seconds to heat up."

Tenshi bowed slightly. "Thank you."

He pointed his thumb over his shoulder. "There should be a spare flight suit somewhere. I'll put it out for you."

She bowed again.

Ellis waited until she was inside the bathroom and the shower was running before he grabbed the fallen locker and flipped it over. The door was missing. One torn hinge still clung to the locker. The other was missing, along with the locker's contents. He couldn't remember most of what was in there. Only the wooden cigar box really mattered, and it was gone, taking his medicine with it.

He picked up the shirt that had been trapped beneath the locker, hoping the box was beneath it. There was a corner of the poster but that was all. The shirt was ripped. He tried to summon up the anger to tear it apart, but in the end, he just balled it up and threw it into the corner of the room.

The ship gave a slight shudder, and he tensed. When the patch on the wall didn't fall off, exposing him to the vast expanse of space, Ellis let out a slow breath and looked at the bathroom door. A dozen questions filled his mind, but he forced them away. It didn't matter who she was, or how she'd come to return from the dead. Maybe she was just a stowaway or had been in a deep coma or something.

The important thing was that she was there. He already felt calmer, just knowing she was close by. He felt fine at the moment, but the withdrawal would come. When it did, she'd help him get through it, he was sure of it.

~*~

Ellis had meant to go straight to the airlock to grab one of the flight suits for Tenshi, but instead he went back to the cargo hold. He tapped the control panel, and the door slid open, but he hesitated before going in. He still wasn't sure he wanted to know how Tenshi had ended up walking around the ship. The lighting panel was still out, but he could see the silhouette of pod fifteen with its lid propped beside it. A nervous feeling settled in the pit of his stomach.

"Stop being an idiot. She's just a stowaway."

He forced his feet to carry him into the hold. The door hissed closed behind him. He had to resist the urge to turn around and make sure it was going to open again when he was ready to leave. Two more lighting panels had died, creating fresh patches of darkness. He chose a route that would take him to pod fifteen without passing beneath the broken LEDs.

His footsteps echoed around the bay as he walked between the pods. He checked the panels as he passed. All of them were sealed, apart from number fifteen. The lid had been removed and propped against the side of the pod. The LED on the control panel glowed red in the darkness. The lid was unmarked. No scratch marks, no broken fingernails, no smears of blood where its inhabitant had fought to escape.

For some reason, he'd expected to find the pod interior lined with silk cushioning, but what he found made a lot more sense. It contained a dense, foam material with a shape cut into it—the shape of a human body. From its size, Tenshi would fit in the cutout perfectly. It was probably custom made to protect her body from damage if the container was dropped or otherwise mistreated.

The sensors that monitored the pod's internal state were at the foot of the container—two discrete black rectangles. Ellis pulled them up and out. The wiring seemed intact, and there were no obvious signs of damage. The foam insert was fine, too. It was as though Tenshi had simply woken up, pushed the lid off her pod, and calmly climbed out.

~*~

Ellis sat in the pilot's chair, his fingers tapping against the armrest. The soft rush of the shower faded away and a few seconds later, with a click, the bathroom door opened. He'd laid out a clean flight suit he'd retrieved from the airlock. It would be too big, but it was better than the clothes Tenshi had been... What had she been? She hadn't been buried; that wouldn't happen until the ship reached Kiran. Entombed? No, that wasn't right.

He shook his head, trying to ignore the resurfacing questions. The techs could work out what had gone wrong once they landed. In the meantime, he'd make Tenshi feel comfortable. She could have his quarters, and he'd rig up a bed of some sort. He wouldn't sleep much without his medicine, anyway.

The door to his room slipped open. Tenshi stepped onto the bridge. Her hair was still a little damp and clung to her shoulders. He'd been right: the jumpsuit was a little too big. But she'd rolled up the sleeves and pulled the belt tight around her waist.

She smiled at him. "Thank you. I feel... human again."

"Great. I have some rations if you're hungry. It's not steak. Well, it says steak on the foil, but it's synthetic." He grimaced. He was stumbling over his words like a lovestruck teenager.

"That would be nice."

Tenshi's eyes sparkled. The shower seemed to have revitalized her, and her skin had lost its unhealthy edge. She still looked nervous, but it no longer seemed like she was about to run away and seal herself behind the airlock.

Ellis found himself staring at her. The resemblance had been uncanny enough in the photograph but in real life, it was like looking at his past brought crashing into the present.

Forcing himself to look away, he pulled a pair of metallic pouches from a cupboard beneath the control panel. He squeezed and shook them both, then handed one to Tenshi. "It takes a couple of minutes to heat up."

They stood in awkward silence for thirty seconds before Ellis hurriedly slipped off the pilot's seat. "Please, sit down, you're probably tired."

"No, I'm fine. Thanks."

They stood, the uncomfortable silence returning until Ellis said, "Lisa, what's the status of the ship?"

Repairs are progressing at the expected rate. Current estimate for a return to full operating capacity is twenty-one hours, forty-three minutes. Margin of error plus/minus nine percent.

"What's the status of the external sensor array?"

A detailed examination of collision damage has determined that in situ repairs are not feasible. I have adjusted the undamaged sensors to compensate with limited results.

He rubbed his forehead. That was bad. "Is it safe for us to get moving again?"

Forward scanning abilities fall below approved minimum levels.

"Any way you can get them above minimum levels?"

Negative.

"So... we either float here in the middle of space until someone finds us or we starve to death, or we carry on and risk hitting more space debris and being sucked out into—"

Suddenly realizing he wasn't alone on the ship any more, Ellis stopped talking. He looked at Tenshi.

She smiled hesitantly. "It's okay. I understand the risks."

"You've been on a spaceship before?"

"Yes, my father was a pilot."

The words caught in Ellis' mind and set off a dozen leaps of logic that all ended at one impossible point. "On Denia?"

"Yes, he worked for Trisense."

More leaps of logic.

"Worked?"

Tenshi seemed to puzzle over her reply. "I haven't seen him for a few years."

Ellis could feel the heat from his food through the foil packaging. He wanted to ask Tenshi her father's name, but he was terrified of the answer. He'd have to ask eventually, but not yet. Instead, he retrieved a couple of sporks from the cupboard and handed one to Tenshi. She tore the top off her packet and squeezed it to open the end so that she could get to the food. The sight reminded Ellis of the envelopes that were now drifting out there in space somewhere. Thankfully, there was still no tinnitus and no headache.

He opened his own packet and shoveled a sporkful of food into his mouth. The synthesized meat was powdery and drenched in spices to hide the bland flavor, but he was suddenly very hungry and the protein was welcome.

They ate in silence. Tenshi's face was unreadable. She was acting as though she escaped from a coffin and found herself stranded in space every day. The same couldn't be said for Ellis. Her comments had set his mind racing, and the ideas it was churning out swung wildly between terrifying and exhilarating.

By the time they'd finished eating, he'd decided to ask her the names of both her parents, that way he could be sure.

But she spoke first. "Who was the woman on the screen? The other one I mean."

The question brought Ellis' thoughts to a screeching halt. "She… err." It was a simple question with a simple answer, but he struggled to find the words.

"Forgive me, you don't need to answer that."

"No, it's… it's okay. She's my daughter. Was my daughter."

Tenshi looked up at the now black screen as though the images were still there. Ellis could almost hear the thoughts whirring in her mind.

She looked back at him. "She's no longer alive?"

"No."

"What happened to her?"

"She was shot, accidentally, during a robbery."

This was usually where people expressed their sympathy for his loss, but Tenshi just tilted her head as though she was puzzled. "Is that why you're traveling to Kiran?"

Ellis started to say no, she'd died five years ago, but he stopped. He didn't remember telling Tenshi where they were going.

Tenshi dropped her eyes. "I'm sorry, that was unacceptable."

"No, no. It's fine."

Ellis searched for a way to change the subject and, without thinking, asked the question that he'd been too afraid to voice. "You said you father was a pilot for Trisense. What was his name?"

She didn't reply immediately. Her brow furrowed as though she was trying to think of the answer to his question.

Ellis' heart quickened in the silence. When she did speak, the words knocked his world off its axis.

"Ellis Osako."

He clutched the edge of the control panel as a heady cocktail of emotions flooded his system—excitement, delight, fear, confusion. His eyes widened, and he stammered, trying to find something to say. "What?"

The word came out hard, sharp. It must have scared Tenshi because she took a step backward.

He held up his hands. "No, don't—I just." He reined in his rampaging emotions. "What did you say his name was?"

"Ellis Osako…"

The breath disappeared from his lungs. He felt his knees loosen and sat down in the pilot's seat before he collapsed completely.

Tenshi's face was still filled with concern. She seemed about ready to bolt. "I'm sorry."

"No, it's not your fault." He fought to find the right words again. Could he have been wrong, all this time? "What's your mother's name?"

Tenshi looked dubious, but she replied anyway. "Himari"

His world tilted again.

"When were you born?"

She frowned and inched toward the door.

Ellis tried to steady his voice. "Your birthday, when is your birthday?" His hands were shaking, but it wasn't the withdrawal this time. If she said—

"May. The thirtieth."

With those three words, the doubt in Ellis' mind evaporated. He didn't know how it was possible and wasn't sure he *wanted* to know, but Tenshi was, somehow, the daughter he thought had been killed.

He laughed. "It's you, it's really you."

"I don't understand."

"I'll show you. Lisa, bring up the *Sept54* video again." He pointed toward the video playing on the screen. "Look, it's you."

Tenshi turned. Her head tilted to one side. The movement was so familiar, Ellis' breath caught in his chest.

She was frowning, though, her head shaking slightly. "It's—I don't know why you're showing that to me."

On the screen, the camera cut to the shot of Lucy standing beside the car.

"Because it's *you*. You must remember going to college?"

She shook her head, but he was sure he could see something in her eyes—like she was trying to dredge up the remnants of a memory from the depths of her mind.

"Think. Try to remember. Your mom and I bought you that car for your nineteenth birthday." God, Himari, what would she say about this? Could they be a family again?

Tears formed in Tenshi's eyes. She blinked them away. "No, I don't understand. I…" She looked at the door leading out of the bridge, toward the cargo hold. "No! I won't."

Ellis reached toward her. "Hey, it's okay."

She looked back at him, confusion and fear filling her eyes. "How did I get on this ship?"

Ellis waved the question away. "It doesn't matter. What matters is that you're here. With me."

The video reached the end and restarted. Ellis heard his wife telling him to leave their daughter alone.

"You said… You said your daughter was killed."

"I thought she—" The words caught in Ellis' throat. "I thought you were, but I was wrong. There must have been a mistake. We'll find out what happened. It doesn't matter, Lucy—"

"That's not my name!"

Tenshi slammed her hand against the control panel to open the bridge door. Ellis leaped from chair and lunged. He caught her arm, but she twisted free as the door slid open and ran down the corridor away from him.

Ellis caught his shoulder on the door frame as he charged after her. "Wait!"

He gained on her quickly, but she reached the cargo hold and slapped the control panel. The door slid open.

"Lisa, shut down access to the cargo hold."

Understood. Access locks activated.

Tenshi slipped inside, just managing to get through before the door closed again.

Ellis slid to a halt in front of the hold. He pressed the open button. The display turned red and there was a short buzzing sound.

"Dammit! Cancel that request."

Understood. Cargo hold access locks deactivated.

Ellis pressed the button again. He was rewarded with a padlock icon and another dull buzz.

Most of the lights in the hold had died, but he could see Tenshi standing on the other side of the door. "Come on, I'm sorry. Let me in."

She stared back at him.

"Lisa, unlock this door."

Access locks are currently deactivated.

"What? That doesn't—" He hammered on the glass. "Please, Tenshi. Open the door and we can talk. I didn't mean to scare you."

Tenshi frowned and shook her head.

Ellis rested his forehead on the door and took a deep breath, trying to calm himself. He needed to take his time. Whatever had happened had left his daughter traumatized, that was clear. He'd freaked her out by unloading this on her without warning. He should have waited, gotten a psychiatrist involved or something. He took a deep breath and raised his head again.

Tenshi was still standing there. She looked so pale and fragile in the semi-darkness. Her eyes were wet with tears.

She spoke.

He couldn't hear her through the door, and he shook his head. "I don't understand."

Her lips moved again, and this time he managed to work out the words. "I can't protect you."

"What do you mean? You can't—"

There was movement behind Tenshi. A dark shape rose up in the gloom. It was humanoid, big and bulky, at least a foot taller than Tenshi and much wider. The figure advanced toward her.

"Look out, someone's in there!"

A second shape, this one smaller, appeared off to Tenshi's right. Ellis couldn't make out any features, but it looked like a woman.

"Lisa, what's going on? Who's inside the cargo hold?"

Cargo hold sensors are currently inoperative. Estimated repair time two hours and three minutes.

"Oh, for God's sake!" He mashed his fingers against the control panel. "Unlock the hold door, now!"

Access locks are currently deactivated.

Now there were four shapes inside the room.

He slapped his palm against the door. "Tenshi! There's someone in there. You have to get out!"

Tenshi gave a slight shake of her head.

He grabbed the edge of the door and tried to pull it open. His fingers slipped, and he fell back. "Dammit!" He punched the window in frustration. The blow sent a thunderbolt of pain down his arm.

The first figure reached Tenshi. It was a young man with a shaved head and pale, glistening skin. His eyes were closed, his mouth pressed into a tight line. His head was tilted slightly, and the bones in his neck pressed against his skin. There was something vaguely familiar about him, but Ellis couldn't place what.

The man moved alongside Tenshi and stopped. He was wearing a white jumpsuit, just as Tenshi had been. Ellis swept his fingers through his hair, then turned and ran to the airlock.

When he got there, the doors seemed intent on holding him back. They crept open, inch by inch as

36

though goading him. As soon as there was a wide enough gap, he pushed himself into the equipment room. It took him a few seconds to open the storage locker, find a toolkit, and fumble with the latch to get it open. The tools inside were old and poorly maintained, but there was a crowbar that looked solid enough. He grabbed it, turned back for a hammer as well, and then ran back to the cargo hold.

The man had been joined by a second, much older man and a woman with long blond hair. They'd stood beside Tenshi. The woman's shoulder brushed against Tenshi's, but she didn't react. She just stared through the glass at Ellis while the others stood there, eyes closed.

More figures appeared out of the darkness.

Ellis let the hammer fall to the floor, then jammed the end of the crowbar into the edge of the door. The metal creaked and groaned as he leaned against it, but the door stayed closed.

Dozens of shadows moved through the room behind Tenshi.

"Lisa, what the hell is going on in there?"

Internal sensors are currently inoperative. Estimated repair time, one hour and fifty-seven minutes.

A girl, maybe twelve years old, walked in front of Tenshi. Part of her head was shaved, and there was a ragged scar running across her scalp. Her head was tilted upward and although, like the others, her eyes were closed, Ellis was sure she was staring at him. The girl's lips curled into a smile.

Ellis swung the crowbar at the window. It bounced off the glass with a sharp crack. He swung again. The tip of the crowbar embedded itself in the window. He pulled it free and fragments of glass tumbled to the floor. He swung the crowbar back again but froze. Another man had appeared and was standing just behind Tenshi. This one Ellis did know. It was the salesman. Marcus.

As Ellis watched, Tenshi placed her hands on the young girl's shoulders.

"What..."

A fresh tear ran down Tenshi's cheek. "I can't protect you."

The surrounding crowd moved forward, led by the young girl. They swarmed past Tenshi toward the door.

There was a beep. The control panel turned green and door slid open.

The girl was through the door before Ellis could react. Her hand snaked out and grabbed him. Ice cold fingers wrapped around his wrist. He twisted free and raised the crowbar. As he brought it down, a man with a broken nose threw his arm in the way. The crowbar thumped against iron hard flesh and almost slipped from Ellis' grip.

The door was too narrow for more than a couple of people to get through at a time, but Ellis could see the figures beyond crowding forward to get to him. Hands grabbed at him. They pulled him forward, toward the hold and its mass of waiting arms. He swung his arms up to knock the girl's hands away. Someone else clutched at his face, hooked fingers grazed his cheek.

Blindly, he swung the crowbar again. It hit something hard, then was wrenched from his grip.

"No!"

Shards of ice wrapped around his ankle. The man with the broken nose collided with Ellis. They fell. Ellis' head cracked against the metal floor. Something hard dug into his back. Fighting to stay conscious, he rammed one arm across the man's chest and pushed. He could feel the chill of the man's skin beneath the thin fabric.

Ellis managed to force the man away and twist sideways. His shoulder caught something hard—the hammer. He grabbed at it. His fingers nudged it farther away, then found the rubber handle. He swung the hammer at the man's head.

It was a glancing blow, but it was enough to knock the man's head sideways. His eyes burst open, his face filled with shock and pain. He let out a high-pitched scream. Ellis pulled the hammer back and swung again. There was a solid crack as it sank into the man's skull. Blood spattered Ellis' face. The man slumped forward, pinning Ellis to the floor.

The crowd in the doorway surged forward.

Ellis felt hands clawing at his thighs. He kicked out, his boots connecting with something fleshy. He pulled the hammer free and swung blindly as he scrambled out from beneath the now still body. Fingernails dug into his ankle. He screamed as agony tore through his Achilles. He kicked again, and the fingers let go.

The girl advanced toward him. Her eyes were still closed, but her smile had turned to a rictus grin that sent fear coursing down Ellis' spine. He got his legs beneath him and, ignoring the pain spiking through his leg, stood. The girl lunged at him. He knocked her hands aside and swung the hammer, but it missed and clanged against the wall.

A dozen people filled the corridor behind the girl. All of them had their eyes closed. All of them were trying to get to Ellis. Except Tenshi. She stood in front of the door, her face filled with sorrow, the mass of people flowing around her.

Ellis threw the hammer at the girl and ran.

"Lisa, open the door to the bridge and start evacuation procedures!"

The hammer clattered to the floor. Ahead, the bridge door slid open. The light in the corridor turned red.

Emergency evacuation procedure initiated. Priming sequence complete in fifteen seconds.

Ellis could hear the crowd behind him, the rustle of their jumpsuits, the slap of bare feet on the metal floor. He didn't look back.

Priming sequence complete in ten seconds.

The bridge seemed to be retreating with every step he took, but then he was inside and slamming his hand against the control panel. The door hissed closed behind him. He jabbed the lock button. The display turned red and a padlock icon appeared. Seconds later, he heard the dull thump of hands hitting metal.

Priming sequence complete in five seconds.

Ellis turned and leaned against the door. He squeezed his eyes closed, trying to force the image of Tenshi, of Lucy, from his mind. It clung to him, suffocating his thoughts. His heart was pounding, and he could hear the rush of blood in his ears.

Priming sequence complete.

A new voice made Ellis start. "I will, mom. I promise."

He turned to look at the main display. The video was still playing. His wife was hugging their daughter.

Ellis clenched his jaw. He was safe now. He'd pull himself back from fight or flight and find a way to get to Tenshi.

"Lisa, what's the status on the internal sensors?"

Currently inoperative. Estimated repair time, one hour and fifty-one minutes.

"Anything you can do to speed that up?"

All options for expedited repair have been exhausted.

The thudding against the door stopped. The sudden silence did nothing to ease Ellis' concerns. He rubbed the bridge of his nose, trying to release the tension that was forming there.

His daughter's words filled the bridge again. "Oh yeah, the old man wants a hug too."

"Kill the video."

The display turned black.

A metallic grinding sound came from somewhere beneath Ellis' feet.

"Lisa?"

Yes, Pilot?

"Did you—"

The control panel beside the door turned green, and the padlock disappeared. The door creaked and shifted slightly.

"Launch evacuation! Now!"

Launch initiated.

There was heavy clunk. The floor began to vibrate, and the roar of the bridge capsule's launch system filled the air. Ellis dived toward the pilot's chair. His fingers touched the armrests, and then he was thrown backward as the capsule launched. He slid across the floor and slammed into the back wall. His teeth clacked together, cutting his cheek.

He felt the bridge tilt forward. The launch system fell silent. That meant they'd cleared the ship. He fought to remember the emergency protocol. Did he have to initiate the distress signal? His thoughts were muddy and sluggish, scrambled by the blow he'd taken.

The capsule tilted again. He could see the chair a few feet away, but his vision was blurry. His head was pounding. Thick waves of pressure pulsed from his forehead. He reached toward the pilot's chair, but it seemed to recede as though it was actually pulling away from him. He dropped his hand to the floor and let darkness wash over him.

~*~

Ellis felt the capsule juddering first. The rest of his senses followed one by one. The faint scent of oil and grease from the metal grille his face was resting on. The taste of blood in his mouth. The outline of the pilot's chair against the glow of the control panel. The subtle, high-pitched whine in his skull.

Groaning, he rolled onto his back. His head was pounding, and when he reached up and touched his forehead, he found a lump the size of a golf ball that was tender to the touch. Blood was crusted beneath his nose.

"Lisa?"

His voice was dry, and for a moment, he thought the ship couldn't hear him.

Yes, Pilot.

"Status."

Evacuation capsule successfully detached three hours and nineteen minutes ago. Environmental support systems are currently operating at eighty-nine percent efficiency. Emergency beacon has been deployed.

Evacuation capsule? Memories reordered themselves inside Ellis' mind until they'd assembled into a mostly chronological version of the events of the last few hours. He tried to sit up, but the sudden movement sent a wave of nausea crashing over him.

When the bridge had stopped spinning, he got unsteadily to his feet, walked to the pilot's seat, and sat down. Half of the lights on the control console had gone dark.

"What's the status of the Redhawk?"

Range to Redhawk seven thousand, eight hundred, and twenty-three kilometers. Telemetry link is intact. Auxiliary computing systems are operating at ninety-one percent capacity.

"What about the repairs?"

Current estimate for a return to full operating capacity is seven hours, thirty-one minutes. Margin of error plus/minus six percent.

The ship was still out there. Tenshi was still out there. Pain pulsed in the center of his forehead. He pressed his fingers against its origin.

"Are the sensors back up?"

Yes, Pilot.

The image of her standing in the doorway, people crowding past her to get to him, flared in his mind. No. They weren't people; they were something else.

"Do a sweep of the entire ship for life signs."

Understood.

Seconds passed.

No lifeforms detected.

"Recalibrate and re-scan."

No lifeforms detected.

Ellis's heart sank. "Any damage to the ship? Depressurization?"

The ship's hull is intact. Environmental support systems are functioning correctly.

He frowned. "Run diagnostics on the cargo hold."

There was a pause that seemed to drag on forever.

Cargo hold status is within normal operating parameters. Hermetic seals are intact.

"That can't be right. Recalibrate and check the seals again."

Again, there was a delay, longer this time.

Hermetic seals are intact.

"All of them?"

Yes, Pilot.

"Isolate pod fifteen and re-scan."

Understood.

Ellis started at the control panel. The cargo hold status LEDs were dark.

Pod fifteen is intact.

"That can't be right."

All sensor banks are operating at ninety-eight percent efficiency. The likelihood of multiple errors occurring is less than point zero zero three percent.

"Bring up the records for pod fifteen."

The display came to life, and the image of Tenshi appeared. Tears blurred Ellis' vision. He swallowed.

"Take us back to the Redhawk."

The evacuation capsule is not equipped with a propulsion system. Emergency beacon has been deployed.

Anger welled up inside him. "Then bring the ship to us."

The Redhawk is not equipped with remote piloting facilities.

Ellis let out a bitter laugh. He tipped his head back and closed his eyes. Tears escaped their corners and trickled down his face. The tinnitus rose in volume briefly, then faded again.

"Any response to the emergency beacon?"

Negative.

"How long will this thing keep me alive?"

Elimination of all non-critical systems will provide enough power to maintain environmental support for three hundred and seventy-one hours.

"So, two weeks?"

Correct.

A dull ache pulsed between Ellis' eyes. "Access my personal files and play file *Sept54*. Full screen."

Pilot, the additional drain on energy reserves will reduce environmental support longevity by—

"Just play the video."

The picture of Tenshi faded away and an image of a box filled car took its place. A young woman was forcing a sleeping bag into the car's trunk.

Ellis smiled. "Are you sure you're taking enough stuff, Lucy?" he said, his words drowning out the tinnitus growing inside his skull.

~*~

Cosmic Jury Duty
Ernie Howard

~*~

"Found this one freezing in the park. Got us a human popsicle."

Stasha always hated when the medics who brought homeless into the ER referred to them as if they were less than human. She understood they dealt with these types of people daily, but she still thought it was no reason to lose their humanity.

"That's enough, Robbie. Everyone came into this world a baby, optimistic when they were young. Even you, Robbie," Stasha said, flashing the paramedic a sarcastic smile.

"Not me. I always wanted to clean the streets and get puked on by random hobos."

Stasha was getting irritated. "Did he puke on you?"

"Not yet, but we have all night," Robbie said.

"I'll take it from here. Thanks."

Stasha grabbed the end of the gurney as Ralph, the biggest man in the hospital, grabbed the other side. Ralph shot Robbie a look that would burn through steel.

Robbie's smug smile melted from his face like ice cream on a hot sidewalk in the summer.

Ralph helped push the homeless man into the room where they kept the not so urgent crowd—where they kept most of the homeless that came in, and the occasional hypochondriac with the sniffles. Stasha had been an ER doctor long enough to know the man wasn't critical, he was just cold.

She bent down to consider the man's eyes. Her small flashlight beam pointed down into some of the bluest eyes she had ever seen. He wasn't disheveled like most of the people that Stasha had seen come through in her five years as an ER doctor. His clothes were clean, without holes. The thin t-shirt and jeans were inappropriate for the cold weather, though.

The man moved his hand quickly, grabbing Stasha's arm in midair. "We have to get back," he said. "I've almost screwed it up." Even though the man's blue eyes burned fiercely, Stasha didn't panic. Her arm had been grabbed by many a patient. The best thing to do in this situation was to stay calm.

"Where do we need to get back to?" Stasha asked. She had decided to go along with whatever the man said. She wanted him to think they were just having a friendly conversation, rather her grilling him with questions.

"We need to get back to the park."

Most homeless people didn't want to leave the hospital. Hot meals and warm beds felt better than cold concrete. This guy wanted to get right back out there. "We've got to get you warmed up first. Can you tell me your name?"

The man rolled his eyes and let go of Stasha's hand. He settled back into the gurney with a sigh. "Marteen."

"Okay, Marteen, my name is Stasha." The man

nodded. "I'll get you all set up, so we can get back to the park."

"We need to get back to the park." The man's teeth chattered in between sentences. "I need to complete my duty. We need to get started, we are falling behind the rest. We can't miss our window."

Stasha let Marteen talk. It was always better if you let them talk. He didn't have the characteristics of a mentally ill person. Not only the clean clothes, but the man's teeth were clean and without rot. Most schizophrenics did not take care of their teeth. Stasha kept going with the conversation.

"Why do we need to get back?" Stasha said as she worked. His pulse and blood pressure were both elevated, but still within the normal range.

Marteen turned his head away from Stasha and looked out the window. "You have to complete your duty to the universe. Please. It's my last task. It has been such a long week."

That sealed the deal for Stasha. The man was a classic crazy. But she was curious where Robbie the ass had picked him up. She might still catch him if she tried now. "I need to leave for a second. I'll be back and bring you some food." The man turned his head from the window. Stasha got up and ran out of the room and down the long hallway to the front of the ER. She was almost to the big double doors when the vibration started. It started off as a hum in her ears but got to where her body was shaking. The walls of the hallway seemed to move back and forth, making Stasha want to throw up. The vibration reached a point where it was too hard to stand up, and Stasha crumpled to the floor. She tried her best to keep her lunch in her stomach, but it came up and splashed on the floor in front of her. She was almost to the point of not being able to take it anymore when the vibration stopped. Stasha sat panting, looking at a puddle of soup that had once been in her stomach.

Stasha wiped her mouth with the back of her sleeve, leaving a dark smear on the clean white jacket. She collected herself. The vertigo and queasiness were gone as quickly as they had come. She felt good, which was surprising compared to only a moment ago, when she'd been spewing her lunch on the floor.

"What the hell was that?" she said. Stasha looked up when she didn't get an answer, towards the nurse's station. No one was sitting in the chair or standing around the desk that was usually abuzz with people looking at charts or answering phones that never stopped ringing. Stasha crawled on her hands and knees to the other side of the desk. The head charge nurse was lying under the front desk. Her leg was slung over the desk chair as if she got tired and needed to put her feet up. Stasha scanned the area. The people she'd passed in the hallway only a moment ago lay strewn on the floor. Everyone lay at odd angles, with arms and legs twisted in unnatural positions.

Stasha moved closer to the person under the desk. It was Gina, the head nurse. She reached out to check the lady's pulse. Her skin was ice cold, and Stasha felt no heartbeat. She quickly tried to push the woman over to begin C.P.R. but her body wouldn't budge. It was like the woman was made of concrete. Stasha pushed back and sat staring at the woman's face. It was frozen, staring off into space.

"She's not dead. Just frozen for a bit."

Stasha spun around and saw Marteen standing above her. The man had a playful smirk on his face, as if he knew an inside joke and he wasn't about to share it with

Stasha.

"What the hell is going on? Who the hell are you?" Stasha said.

"I told you. We need to do our duty. It's time to go back to the park." Marteen's smirk changed to a beaming smile. "You need to come with me, you are chosen."

Stasha rubbed her head. One minute the world made sense to her. The next, she was trying to find a pulse on a woman whose skin had the consistency of a sidewalk. She got up and followed Marteen who was almost to the double doors. He stopped and looked back at Stasha. She moved forward in a trance. Her body betrayed her even as her mind tried to make sense of all that was happening.

The wrongness of everything went into full throttle as Stasha stepped outside. Sunlight had an artificial quality. The color of everything was off. Robbie the paramedic stood frozen in what looked like mid-sentence with a police officer Stasha had seen around the hospital a couple of times. She looked up at the sky. It had a weird bluish film painted on it. An airplane sat suspended in the air high in the atmosphere, its contrail not getting any longer and not dissipating in any way. About ten feet from her head, a pigeon was frozen mid-flight. A petrified worm dangled from its mouth. Stasha had been so caught up in looking at all the weirdness her reality had become that she hadn't realized Marteen was already half way down the block, making his way to the park he had almost frozen in. Stasha realized then it wasn't cold. The air had a piped in feel like at the hospital. Not too cold, and not too hot, just right.

Stasha jogged to get on pace with Marteen.

"It's a lot to take in. What you thought was normal, your grasp on how things work, has been turned upside down." The man looked down at her. The amused smirk had come back. "Right?"

Stasha didn't know what to say. Her words seemed stuck in her throat. "I don't... How..."

Marteen put his hand up and shook his head in a knowing way. "I was like you only a week ago; I sold insurance. This woman walks into my office saying I have been chosen and that I need to come with her. I take one look at her dirty clothes and tell her to get out of my office. Then I feel the vibration and everyone turns into popsicles. I understand what you're feeling. I'll explain more when we get to the park."

The park was only two blocks away, but when they arrived, Stasha felt like she had walked two miles. Her brain felt like it was misfiring even though her body kept going. Marteen walked up to a pedestal that sat in the middle of a soccer field. *What a weird place to put something like this.* Seemed like it would be bad for games.

Marteen pushed down on the top of the pedestal and the vibration she'd felt a little while ago came back. This time, it was different, though. It didn't feel like it was in the air; this felt manmade, coming from underground. Stasha stared at Marteen with a look of horror.

"It's okay. I'm just engaging the view screen."

Once again, Stasha looked at Marteen like he was crazy. "The view screen?" Stasha said. She noticed she was clutching herself, waiting for the next reality-breaking episode to happen.

A loud boom knocked Stasha to the ground. Two long poles came out of the dirt in front of the pedestal. They were skinny at first, rising into the sky. As they went, the base got bigger and bigger until the poles were at least a hundred feet in the sky. Marteen looked back at where Stasha was sitting. "Just the display screen," he said.

Marteen pushed one more button and a blue screen

appeared in between the two poles. He pushed back from the pedestal and sat next to Stasha. Stasha scooted away from him. Nothing—not the first time she'd cut someone open, or the first time she had ever subdued a crack head—could compare with what she felt at this moment.

"Okay. I would assume you have questions?" Marteen said. He had lost the smirk, and now he just looked concerned.

"Do I have questions? What do you think? In less than a half hour my world has become a Sci Fi movie." Stasha shook her head and looked away. She had been rubbing her forehead for the last half hour, and when she put her hand up to rub some more, she winced. Her hand came away with a red tinge to it.

"I can only tell you what I know. And I have a short time to do it. In a few minutes, I will be frozen and asleep just like that fellow over there." Marteen pointed to a man lying on his side. His face frozen in a smile, and his hands frozen in mid throw. What looked like a dog statue lay close by. "I can only know this by what Trac told me. The memory of him is gone. But I remember what I am supposed to tell you. The being on the screen will tell you what to do. I am here to complete my mission. To set you up for success." Marteen paused and looked up at the screen high above their heads. It flickered. "Trac's almost ready." He turned back to Stasha. "The Earth, to you or anyone else, has always been a planet. A good one, perfect for supporting life. Life with energy. People or beings each with their own pocket of energy. Think of small batteries. The earth has to use these batteries for energy to fulfill its true purpose. For what it was made for."

"What is it made for?" Stasha's voice came out of her throat as a croak.

"It's a safety mechanism. A spaceship. It's a weapon," Marteen said.

"A weapon against what?"

Marteen grabbed Stasha's hand. His grip tightened, and he fell back into the grass. "It's a weapon against…" Marteen puked in the grass. With his other hand, he wiped his mouth. "It's a weapon against other universes. It keeps them, uhhhhh."

The man froze before Stasha's eyes. His mouth formed an O, and his vice grip hand let go and curled into a fist. Stasha nudged the man with her foot, but couldn't budge him.

The giant screen popped on once again. It displayed an insignia like none other she'd ever seen. Some creature wrapped around a hexagon that looked like a shield. The image was foreign and familiar at the same time.

Stasha stared up at the screen, frozen like the surrounding people. It popped a few times and then another image displayed itself.

The being looked human, and if it hadn't been for its long pointed ears and giant head, it could have passed for an average person on the street. It opened its mouth, exposing a green tongue.

"Slur per Der, slur per dur," it said.

Stasha looked on, confused but fascinated. This was an alien from another planet. Coming to her live and no one was around to see it. The thing smiled and let out with a banshee shriek that made the sound feedback in speakers she couldn't see. Stasha covered her ears.

"I'm sorry, chosen one of Earth. You would think after doing this for billions of years I wouldn't forget that beings of Earth don't speak Shwanzak!" The being smiled again and let out with little squeaks and squawks. It slapped the table, finding this whole exchange very amusing. "I am Tractopedial, but you can call me Trac for short. Or General Trac, if you are more formal." Stasha's mind gave in.

She couldn't help but smile. The alien seemed good hearted. Out of the whole universe she had found the dorky alien that laughed at his own jokes.

"Do you have questions for me?" Trac said.

Now it was Stasha's turn to laugh. She threw up her hands and shook her head. She saw that Trac was still smiling, but he looked a little disgusted.

"I don't think I will ever get used to you humans laughing. Sounds like two flactracs singing on a blactrac." Trac made a face like a kid who was forced to eat his peas. "Anyway, I'm sure your predecessor filled you in on your cosmic duty."

"No, he did not. What is all this? What duty?" Stasha said. She thought she would be more nervous to talk to an alien, but Trac seemed nice enough.

"Ah strac! It is so hard to find good help in the universe these days. Just a few duties ago, I had a Heliospec that did not understand how to even control his spaceship." Stasha looked at Trac, confused once again. "To use one of your phrases, human, UGH! Your spaceship is your ah... What term do you use...? Your planet. And you will need to learn to fly it to catch up with the other planets that started their journey. "Yes," Trac looked down at his wrist that glowed blue. "About five Earth-minutes ago. So, if you please..." Trac pointed toward the podium. Stasha got up from the grass and walked over to the podium. The surface had just looked smooth while she was sitting in the grass, but as she got closer, she could see what looked to be a touch screen with what looked like the apps on her phone.

"I know! I have been trying to get the Universe

defense fund to upgrade the equipment on Earth for years, but there are just no funds for defending one universe from another. So, we will have to make due."

Stasha would say the controls looked very advanced, but she didn't want to sound stupid. Instead, she just shook her head yes and smiled.

"Okay. See that blue button on your right side?"

Stasha's hand hovered over a red button. At the moment, she couldn't figure out her left from her right.

"No! Not the red button. That comes later."

Stasha jumped back from the touch screen.

"Sorry to scare you. But don't touch that button right now. Now, as they say on your planet, your other right." Trac let out with another one of his shrieks. "Oh shraptac! That never gets old."

Stasha looked up at the screen, not trying to hide the annoyance in her face.

"Right back to business. The blue button on your right. Tap it. This will disengage the download. You are about to learn more in 3 seconds than you have learned in your short human life. Ready?" Trac said.

"I guess." Stasha said. She tapped the blue button on the screen and a holograph of what looked like a helmet surrounded her head. "Oh, this is cool!"

"You humans… So amused by such archaic things. Strac, strac, strac." Trac slapped the top of his desk once again. "Are you ready?"

Stasha didn't know what to be ready for, but she shook her head yes. "I'm ready."

"Press the yellow button in the middle of the screen, please," Trac said.

Stasha's finger hovered over the yellow button. If her reality hadn't gone out the window, she might have waited longer to press the button. But the saying "What do I have to lose?" was the mantra of the day. Stasha pressed the button, and the hologram hummed to life, and she felt a slight tinkle that rotated around her skull. An image filled her head, and she realized what she was seeing. The start of her universe. There was no bang. The universe just was. The images came faster and faster, until she couldn't keep up with them. She saw that this was the way it always was. This was how humans had always insured life in this universe. They've always had to protect it. She realized humanity had never been alone. The helmet hummed louder, almost to the point of it being painful, and then stopped. Stasha pressed the blue button, and the helmet disappeared. She knew what she had to do. It was time to defend the universe once again. It was her turn for cosmic jury duty. Or at least that was what they called it. *They* meaning the people who served before her.

Stasha looked down at the panel. Moments before, she did not understand what any of the buttons meant. Now, the panel looked almost juvenile. Like a child's toy. Stasha looked up at the screen and smiled at Trac. "I know what to do now."

Trac smiled. "I know you do. I'll check back in when we get close. Safe travels, being of Earth." Trac saluted Stasha, and the screen went blank.

Stasha sighed and pressed a button she hadn't seen before. It was a picture of the Earth. She pressed it without hesitation. Earth was late to the party, and she had no misgivings after the download. This must happen.

The screen popped on. It was a map. First of satellites, the Solar System, the Milky Way Galaxy, and then the known universe. Large arrows pointed out where not to go. These pointed to giant suns and black holes that would gobble the earth like yesterday's leftovers. It didn't matter. Once they got past the Kuiper belt, Stasha would engage the autopilot. The download had assured her that the Earth was a functioning spaceship, and she had nothing to worry about. Still, a trickle of sweat ran down her forehead as she engaged the propulsion system. There was a grinding noise, and the sky lit up with lights pointing the way. She looked behind her, the moon was following behind like a rusty muffler dragging on the street.

Moving the planet was easy. Getting around the things in the way was the hard part. She looked up at the sky and saw a light burn up in the atmosphere. The panel squawked to life with a robotic female voice. "Satellite terminated. Please try to be careful, Earthling."

"Whoops," Stasha said. The grin on her face was ear to ear. She wished she could take out a few more, but she had things to do.

Stasha engaged the artificial atmosphere and prepared to see what this old girl could do. She pressed a brown button and a throttle lever popped out from the side of the podium. Stasha grabbed it. This time, her hand wasn't shaking. She pushed it forward, and the world shuddered a little. The thrusters bogged down a bit when she got close to Jupiter. The large planet's gravitational pull threatened to crash the Earth into its surface, but the Earth chugged along like an old diesel train.

Once Stasha realized she was past the Kuiper belt, she pushed the lever all the way forward. It was like watching a light show. Stars became white lines, and small bits of whatever was in front of the earth popped in the sky like fireworks. She watched for a little while and then engaged the auto pilot. The Earth hummed along at an even clip. Stasha went to find something to eat.

She woke up next to the pedestal the next day. She'd

fallen asleep in the grass. The air outside was warm, and she thought it would be a good idea not to stray too far away from the controls. Stars still zoomed by. She had no idea just how far she had traveled, but she figured it was quite a distance. The light show become less dense. Dread crept up into her body. The download hadn't explained just what she would face at the edge of the universe. What was it they had to defend the universe against? Marteen explained it as another universe. But what was that? Was it a black hole? An army of interdimensional pirates?

"Earth being!" The screen popped to life, and Trac appeared. He was smiling his weird alien smile. "How was your slumber?"

"Good. Thank you, Trac."

Trac looked pleased. "We are almost at our destination. If you would pull the lever back to cruising speed, I would like to go over some protocols."

Stasha did what she was asked. The Earth made a grinding noise like an old Chevy, and the stars halted in front of her. Another planet, visible in the sky, matched the Earth's speed. Its atmosphere was green with black continents that lay inside patches of the green sky.

"I have been cruising along with you all along," Trac said.

"I didn't even notice you, Trac," Stasha said. She was surprised.

"Yes, my planet has a cloaking device. I have always been assigned to the Earth. I've gotten the pleasure of watching you odd humans for years. Bickering and fighting with each other, about such small things…" Trac looked up as if pondering something. "Guess that's a conversation for another time. Anyway, if you will look to the left of your sky, you will see a small cluster of planets." Stasha looked and saw thirty tiny pinpoints of light in formation. "As you can see, there is a spot missing right in the middle. That is where you will park your planet." Trac looked down at her. Stasha could tell he was making sure she understood.

"I got it, Trac," Stasha said.

"Well then, steady as she goes!"

Stasha nudged the lever forward a little, and the pinpoints of light quickly got bigger. She was just about there when she eased off the lever and slid the Earth into its space.

Greetings from all the other planets came in, but Stasha couldn't understand what any of them said. She registered a short hello and then turned communication off.

"What now, Trac?" Stasha said.

"Now we wait." Some of the amusement had gone out of his voice, and Stasha knew it was time to get to work. "Shouldn't take long. It usually doesn't. What I need you to do now is engage the pusher."

Stasha knew what Trac was talking about because of the download, but she still felt she needed to be sure. "The red button?" Stasha said.

Trac looked down at her. "Yes, earthling, the red button."

Stasha's hand hovered for a second over the button, and then she pressed it.

Marteen and the rest of the people in the park stood up all at once. Stasha couldn't suppress the scream that came out of her mouth. Every one that had been in the park had stood up all at once. Their heads tilted up to the sky with their mouths open.

"The weapon is engaged. When you see it, and you will know what it is, press the red button once more,"

Trac said.

Stasha looked out into the dark abyss where time and space was born and saw nothing for a few seconds. And then she saw the swirl. It was a peach color. It took up almost the whole sky and was getting bigger. For a second, Stasha didn't know what she was looking at. Then she realized it was an enormous fingertip cutting through the fabric of her universe. Her heart beat so fast, she felt like it would pop out of her chest. She quickly pressed the red button once more. Blue energy shot out of the people's mouths in the park, and she could see trails of light coming from all parts of the city, and what she assumed was the rest of the world. There was a hum that turned into a whine that broke into an earth-shattering scream. Stasha felt like her body would come apart. The light from the rest of the world and the other worlds converged into a point in space, gathering power. The beam blasted out and towards the finger and pushed.

Stasha blacked out.

"Earthling… Earthling… Stasha!"

Stasha opened her eyes that felt like she'd washed them in beach sand. She sat up and looked around. The people in the park were back to being statues.

"Don't worry, you are not alone. No human being can stand the force of seven billion of your kind screaming all at once." Trac smiled. "The finger is gone for now. You are back, orbiting around your sun. You have completed your cosmic duty." Trac stood up and clapped. Stasha's mind felt beat up.

"How long has it been?" Stasha said.

"About one and half Earth days. I tugged you and your moon back," Trac said

Stasha rubbed the sides of her face. "All that because of a finger," Stasha said.

"What!" Trac looked hurt. "A giant finger from another universe that could destroy ours. Yes, all that."

Stasha felt dumb all of a sudden and contemplated what she had seen.

"Don't try to wrap your head around it. You will forget it anyway once you do one more task. Push the side of the pedestal where it says freeze."

Stasha looked to the side of the pedestal. The word freeze written in white block letters stood out. She pushed it. Displaying a little button and a timer.

"You must pass the task on to the next chosen one. Her name is Jordan Grant, she lives at 9810 Violet Street, about three blocks from here. Set your timer for two hours. You know what to do."

Stasha pushed the button and set the timer. "Thanks, Trac." She smiled up at the alien.

Trac burst out with another one of his shrieks. "Oh, Trac! Trac! Trac! It's my job, you silly earthling! Now go to it. We are already falling behind schedule, and I'll have to educate this one too. The universe is depending on you!"

The giant screen quickly disappeared into the ground. The pedestal retreated as well, waiting for its next servant.

Stasha got moving. The information that was stored in her head seemed to fade away until she felt like she was walking in a dream. All she could think about was 9810 Violet Street; Jordan Grant; the universe depends on it.

~*~

Historic
Paul K. Swardstrom

~*~

"And as humanity reaches for the stars, we will need to have onboard medical care that is ahead of the curve, responsive and available. The Galen Tube will be the means by which this happens."

Jos Rayn stood with a triumphant smile on the stage, smiling his most clever smile for the camera as it blasted out the proceedings to every corner of the earth. It was important for the whole planet to see this—especially the Galen Enterprises stockholders. They'd need a lot more capital in order for this project to really get humming.

More importantly, if this project became a reality, it would go a long way toward cementing Jos Rayn's place in history as an innovator, a man who helped to usher in the next new era of mankind. A man on the scale of Edison, Tesla, or Bill Gates. He would be historic.

Jos pushed on. "In our ongoing quest to push the boundaries of humankind and explore space, The Galen Tube will be a necessary component. But that's not all. With enough refinement, the Galen Tube will be able to slow and even press the pause button on the process of aging. Our goal is for the

Galen Tube to be affordable for use in every home."

At that, the dam broke and every reporter in the room had questions. The clamoring for his attention was deafening. He answered questions from five carefully planted reporters before he thanked the crowd, looked into the camera, thanked everyone listening, and then walked off the stage.

Jos grabbed a bottle of water just offstage, aware that the cameras were still rolling. He smiled and generously shook the hands of those who came to congratulate him before his sister Amalia interrupted to escort him to the car.

Out of the view of the cameras, Jos slumped. He was dog tired at only 10:30 in the morning. Amalia handed him three pills and Jos threw them into his mouth and guzzled the entire bottle of water. He loosened his tie as they continued to walk and wiped his head with a towel proffered by J-me, his AI robot assistant, waiting faithfully by the car.

"That was a good talk, Mr. Rayn," J-me said as it opened the door.

"It better have been, J-me," Jos replied as he sat down and scooted over. "We need that capital to get this project really humming."

Jos turned to his sister. "What's the word from Sandra?"

"They have the working prototype ready for demonstration," she replied.

"Good. Let's go."

She frowned at him. "Are you sure? You're not looking so good."

"I'm sure. I need to put in an appearance to keep them honest. Take me there now, dear sister."

She waved her hand dismissively toward the robot.

"Your request was anticipated, Mr. Rayn," J-me said. "We're already on our way."

Jos sat up from his prone position inside the compartment of the eight-foot-long tube. "It's very comfortable," he noted.

Sandra Ong nodded distractedly, her attention on Amalia's two boys, playing in a Galen Tube mock-up fifteen feet away.

"They'll be okay, Dr. Ong. As long as that thing is inactive, that is."

"Of course, of course," Sandra said. She turned back to Jos. "Anyway, the tube is comfortable, yes. We designed it that way to sustain a human inside of it indefinitely. It needs to be able to hold that person comfortably for the long term. In a non-gravitic environment, it would be even better..." A crash in the corner snagged her attention.

"Tell me more about the trial," Jos implored while Amalia took care of the kids. It was too bad they were along. He'd agreed to bring them along in the limo and make the event earlier part of a family day. It hadn't occurred to Jos that the boys might be in the way here.

"Over the last year," Sandra began, "the Galen Tube has been involved in a variety of medical tests. We've set up workshops in oncology, hematology, urology, cardiology, and infectious diseases, among others. It has even sped up the healing of a broken bone." She pointed at her own arm.

She just broke it last week! There was no sign of the break.

"And your results?" Jos asked.

"So far we've seen that the Galen tube is successful at stopping many diseases in their tracks. Blood diseases and cancers can be treated with it as well. We may not always be able to heal a disease completely, but we can usually stop it from progressing."

"And age reversal?"

"We can rejuvenate cells on a cell by cell basis, Mr. Rayn. Death by aging may soon be a thing of the past."

A chill skittered down his back. This was so exciting, he wanted to share it with someone, but Amalia was off taking care of her kids.

"So, what do we need to do to go wide with this thing?" he patted the side of the tube.

"It needs to go through the testing. A lot of what it needs for final approval now is consistency. Once we apply for FDA approval, it's a ninety-day process."

"And we'd better be damn sure it's ready," Jos interrupted.

"Yes," Sandra responded. "And for use in space, we need to be sure it's self-sustaining."

"Right. So, what do you need from me?" One thing Jos had learned over the years was that there was always a list. Someone always needed something.

Sandra blinked, but responded quickly. "We'd like to do a space trial. That's what we've designed it for, after all."

Jos pursed his lips. That could get expensive, but it made sense. "What would that look like?"

"At least one subject in the tube for three months, minimum."

Jos nodded decisively. "All right, I'll look into it. What you're talking about would require a joint venture with Interstellar Enterprises."

Sandra opened her mouth, but stopped herself, a hint of a smile on her lips. "I could always call up Elon," she teased.

"Not funny, Sandra. I'm looking into it," Jos tossed over his shoulder as he headed out the door, following Amalia dragging her two boys by their sleeves.

~*~

Jos sat in the front seat and let Amalia have the back with the boys.

"How was the demonstration, Mr. Rayn?" J-me asked.

"Excellent. I was in there for fifteen minutes and I feel refreshed."

"Good, sir. I trust you are moving ahead with the next phase?"

Jos nodded. "They've tried it out extensively and it's working better than expected. We're ready to move on."

"Congratulations, sir. That sounds like a special achievement."

Jos leaned back and smiled toward the ceiling of the vehicle. "Yes, J-me. Yes, it is special. When the production line gets going, it'll change the whole human race." *It'll be historic.*

Jos pulled up work reports on the pad in front of him. It was turning out to be a good day. The reviews of his presentation were pouring in as overwhelmingly positive. Not only that, but the stock prices were climbing sharply. The news that the Galen tube was ready for the next phase was a welcome and important step.

"Mr. Rayn," J-me interrupted his reverie. "There's something you need to know."

"What is it?" he asked with his eyes closed dreamily.

"Your doctor called and left a message with your office a minute ago. It's about those tests you went through. He wants you to come right in."

~*~

"And you're sure?"

"Yes, Mr. Rayn. It's a rare degenerative blood disorder."

Jos sat in shock. For twenty years, he'd practically ruled the world. Whatever he'd touched had turned to gold. Galen Enterprises was only the last in a long line of multi-billion dollar companies, Interstellar and Robo-Me among them. Although Jos had never counted, he was told that he was one of the fifty richest people on the planet, if he cashed in all of his stock options.

How could this happen? He supposed that this kind of thing could happen to anyone. He just hadn't thought of himself as just anyone in a really long time.

"What's the prognosis?" Amalia asked the doctor.

Doctor Shirav looked intently toward Jos. He was always very direct, a trait that Jos appreciated. It left a little to be desired in bedside manner, however. "You're already feeling the beginning of it," he said. "That's why you came to me. Tiredness, lethargy, numbness. It will progress to circulatory problems. Limbs will begin to respond lethargically, sleep will be difficult yet a constant companion, breathing will become increasingly labored. Within six months, it will be a miracle to see you outside of a chair."

"After that, how long?"

Doctor Shirav shrugged. "It's hard to say. A year from now? Eighteen months? It depends upon the patient."

Jos thought about his options and finally looked his doctor in the eye. "I need to tell you what my company has been working on."

~*~

It was a beautiful solution to a lot of problems, really. Jos Rayn, the wunderkind visionary, would lead the way to the stars via his own long-term flight.

It was planned as a four-month long out and back trip with a bonus dual duty. The ship itself was on an exploratory mission to catch up to a small asteroid—a rock—that was floating through local space. The *Hippocratica* would catch up to the asteroid and record as much data as possible before they passed, and then *Hippocratica* would return to Earth.

Jos Rayn would be the lone passenger on the trip and would experience none of it. He was to enter into one hundred and ten days of stasis inside the Galen Tube, where his blood would be recirculated and regenerated several times a day. A special blend of drugs would enter his system, attaching to and disabling the cells that were causing the degenerative disease. Other parts of the machine would refresh his entire system and keep his muscles from atrophying. He was promised that when he exited the Galen Tube, he would be healthier than he'd been since his mid-twenties.

Amalia Rayn had been handed the keys to the chairmanship of five different companies in the last two days. She watched Jos being plugged into the Galen Tube for launch with her eight-year old son standing by her side.

Jos smiled and gave a thumbs up as the cover came down. He watched as his sister fought tears, struggling to stand strong next to her young son, Galen, the boy who had overcome two bouts of cancer in his own young life.

Jos held out his hand and the cover stopped. He asked Amalia and Galen to come close and gave them both a hug. "It won't be long."

"For you…" Amalia responded.

He smiled. "Of course, but four months should just fly by—especially with as busy as you're about to be."

"You just get home soon, brudder."

"I will."

Amalia turned to go, and he quickly grabbed her arm. "Ama."

She turned back, the tears coming down. "It'll be *historic*," he whispered. He noticed the barest hint of a smile and he let go of her arm.

The cover closed and the technicians finished their jobs. One by one, the people exited the capsule.

~*~

After the rush of launch, he lay in the tube, weightless and waiting. There wasn't much to see, but the ship was in the process of orienting itself toward its objective of catching up to the asteroid while the automated functions of the tube adjusted around him. The technicians in the control center in New Mexico were running a final systems check before they reported in.

"Albuquerque to *Hippocratica*," he heard from a speaker nearby.

"This is Jos Rayn. I hear you."

"All systems are go, Mr. Rayn. You're scheduled to go into forced stasis in two minutes. We will begin the burn towards LAO-02802 soon after that."

Jos took a deep breath. "I'm ready. I'll see you in four months."

"Four months, Mr. Rayn. We'll see you then. Godspeed."

Consciousness faded and everything went to black.

~*~

When consciousness returned, Jos Rayn woke quickly. Finally released from the sleep forced upon him over the last four months, his body felt refreshed and vibrant. He felt where probes and needles had recently left his body. All that was left was the mask attached to his face that allowed him to breathe and be fed. Well, that and the tube attached to the other end.

He tapped the window in front of him and it transformed to a display. He typed in a command, the tube opened, and Jos slipped the mask off his face. He fully disengaged from the machine and floated naked inside his space capsule. He found the compartment that contained his clothing and began the acrobatic dance of putting his clothes on.

Jos paused and allowed himself to just breathe. He felt terrific! The techs had been right. They had to have been right. He couldn't remember his body feeling this good. Just to be sure, he checked the display on the side of the Tube. It reported his blood function at 99.86% normal. Jos reviewed the reports over the last four months. The last detection of the diseased cells occurred five weeks ago, yet treatment had continued unabated in order to be absolutely sure the process would be effective.

He was in remission, which was a major victory. Galen Enterprises would change human history forever with the Galen Tube. Jos finally had cemented the legacy he'd been working for all of these years.

He needed a glass of champagne, but that could wait. First, contact.

He pulled himself into the one chair that was installed in the capsule and strapped in. He keyed the com systems and sent the message: "Albuquerque, this is *Hippocratica*. Come in."

There was no response.

He keyed the com again and sent the message again. And again. He sent the message five times before deciding that something was wrong. Was it the com or something else?

Luckily, every system on the ship was redundant and could be checked against each other. He keyed the alternate com system and tried the message on it while checking to see if it registered on the primary system. The good news was that he heard himself through the primary system. The bad news? No response from Albuquerque.

Jos didn't want to think about the implications, but they were at the periphery of his thoughts. Instead, he got to work.

~*~

It turned out that there was no response from Houston either. Or ESOC, or TsUP Korolyov, or Beijing. Or anywhere, for that matter.

In the hours since his emergence from the Galen Tube, Jos had tried every transmission code on every channel that he had access to. He went through the entire sequence twice, just to be sure.

He'd even tried the transmission codes to the space station and the Mars X mission. Still, nothing.

He willed himself not to panic. After all, panic would get him nowhere, and more likely than anything, dead. At this point, he was flying blind and deaf. Luckily, the command module was preprogrammed with a flight path that included re-entry. Unluckily, he was counting on landing in the water off the California coast. He was beginning to lose hope that his ride was coming to pick him up.

Where was everyone?

He shot a look out the port. Still no view of Earth, except for that speck of brightness that his readout promised him was home. He was still two days away from landing. Jos pulled up the specs on the com unit and started reading. He hadn't had an all-nighter in at least a few years, but he was going to personally check every system. Too bad he wasn't a rocket engineer.

~*~

There. The last recorded transmission was seventy-three days ago. After that, nothing. It was as if Interstellar Enterprises and Galen Enterprises forgot their multi-million-dollar asset floating through space—not to mention Jos himself.

Jos pulled up the final transmission. It contained a video file. Maybe there would be an explanation there. He opened the file and pressed play.

It was Amalia. The picture seemed odd, as if shot through a prismatic lens. She seemed a bit tired and unkempt. Frazzled. "Jos, Honey. We had to go."

She turned and appeared to talk to someone off camera. There was some jostling before she turned back again. "I don't have much time. We've been saved. We didn't know we needed saving, but it turns out we did. We were offered a way out before *IT* came."

Jos didn't like the way she said the word *it*. Something seemed off with her. Her eyes, maybe? Her mannerisms?

"They showed us that the Earth was going to die, that *IT* was coming. We didn't believe at first, but they showed proof after proof. *IT* is coming, Jos. I'm sorry."

She'd started crying, but Jos had seen enough already. Amalia was strong, confident, and he'd never seen her this shaken in all her life, even when her husband had died.

"Jos," she started through her sniffles. "They're taking us with them, but we couldn't do anything about you…" she looked off camera, startled, and said something to whomever it was.

"I have to go. J-Me is on the pickup boat, waiting for you." She placed her hand up to the camera, "Jos, you have to know…" the video stopped playing. Jos checked and rechecked. There was nothing else. He watched the video several times before he collapsed in his seat, just staring at the blank screen.

~*~

Jos lost track of how long he sat in stunned silence.

All his life, he'd been chasing a legacy. Jos Rayn would have been known in every household on Earth. The Galen Tubes would affect the very quality of life itself, even lengthening it significantly. Not a single human being born in the future would have been ignorant of his name and accomplishments.

Now?

What did all that really matter?

The capsule's screens showed the image of a dark Earth. Everyone was gone.

It took a reentry alarm to snap him out of his reverie. He went through the motions of battening everything down and securing himself for reentry. He was ready with three minutes to spare. He had just finished strapping himself in when the entire communication unit lit up, indicating an incoming transmission. *What could that be?* He leaned forward, opened the com, and listened.

"Mister Rayn," the voice started. "Our remote sensors indicate that you are alive and have been actively attempting to communicate with your friends. We trust that by now you have found the message from your sister. We apologize for the inconvenience we have caused. We missed having your company on our long journey through the void. We assure you we will take good care of humanity. Your sister has proven to be delicious company." The transmission ended.

Delicious. What kind of turn of phrase was that? He could imagine someone saying that about an enjoyable party guest, but an alien being?

Delicious...

The roar of re-entry joined voices with Jos as he screamed. During thirty minutes of re-entry, the tiles on the outside of the capsule elevated to temperatures of three thousand Fahrenheit, and Jos' blood boiled along with it. Hot tears burned his eyes, and he allowed the pain to fuel his rage.

Splashdown, and floating. Jos, throat raw and tears blurring his vision, checked all the exterior systems before he popped the hatch. Outside, the sun was shining. Waves lapped against the sides of the capsule. Jos blinked at the brightness and held a hand over his eyes. It was a beautiful day, the conditions outside at odds with the pit eating at him.

J-me would be along in a half an hour. And then what?

Jos looked around. Only human on Earth? Couldn't be. Someone else had to have slipped out of the grasp of the aliens who'd visited while he was in stasis over the last four months. Jos vowed to find them. Together, they would find a way to chase down those that had taken his sister.

Take my people and leave me alive? Mistake. When he was finished with them, the ending would truly be historic.

~*~

The Off World Kick Murder Squad II

Daniel Arthur Smith

~*~

The crew gathered around Anson as he explained the three-dimensional translucent green image hovering above the holo-table. "As you can see," he said, "heavily forested foothills surround the river valley, and in its center, the Korean Syndicate's walled compound: four four-story buildings and a large geodesic sphere."

"Is that a—" Hodge began.

"A Bubble station? Yes. It's a Bubble connecting this plane to the others and, from the intel, a Tube station as well. This small glowing red point suspended in the third floor of the building closest to the Bubble is our target."

"Do they know we're here?" asked Hodge.

"We were lucky," said Anson. "The device brought us in at the cusp of the atmosphere and it appears the Captain's near vertical landing didn't trigger any alarms. I scanned the channels and there's no chatter about us. They're not expecting or looking for anybody. So, no, I don't think the Syndicate knows we're here." Anson spread his hand wide in the air and the holo-table grew in unison until the building holding the red dot was large in front of them. "As I was saying, the target is two thousand klicks away. Right in the middle of structure three."

"Who is it?" asked Hodge.

"Someone called 'Cerulean Blue.' I don't have a picture or description, just the name."

"So we don't know who it is? What they look like?"

"Does it matter?" I asked.

"No. Of course not. I just wondered."

Anson tapped the virtual console and the layout of the building's third floor interior appeared. He continued. "According to the intel, Cerulean is in a cell fortified by two sets of security doors, one on either end of the corridor." He touched the console again and red panels lit up around the target. "They're in a sealed room."

"How about the top? Do we know what's on the floor above?" I asked.

"We don't have that."

"What if we fly in?" asked Bailer.

"Ah," said Anson. He held his hand up and pinched his fingers to his thumb. The image on the table became smaller. He tapped the console again. A dozen places on the wall and across the tops of the buildings lit red. "There are turrets on the rooftops and all along the perimeter wall."

"The turrets, the wall—what are they afraid of?" Cassidy asked. "No one is supposed to even know they're here."

"I don't think the security is for people," said Anson.

"What's that mean?" asked Hodge.

Anson's fingers ran across the console. "I think they're set up to fend off these." This time, a huge, cubed, three-dimensional image of a winged creature floated eye level above the table.

"What's that? Why they afraid of birds? And how come that bird ain't got no feathers?"

"This bird is the size of the Jentu. They're close to a species that disappeared from Earth a few million years ago."

"Then what are they doing here?"

"This planet didn't get the memo," said Cassidy.

"What?"

"This planet was never struck by a meteor," she added.

Hodge was becoming upset. "You mean there's meteors coming too?"

"No," said Cassidy. "It means that mammals never took over the mirror."

Hodge was puzzled. "I thought you said this was no mirror?"

"It's not," I said. "Let's focus here. We can't fly in and out. Can we get in past the wall?"

Anson lit up an iridescent blue trail that led from the Jentu, through the foothills, to the wall. "If we land here at dusk, you can hike it to the compound under cover of darkness. We'll have to shut down the compound's security from the inside, then we can bring the Jentu in for extraction before light."

"Rhia and Rhoe," I said. "You two will need to come. Cassidy, you stay back with Bailer and Anson."

"What about what we heard out there knocking down trees?" asked Hodge. "It was something huge, and it weren't no flying bird."

"Right," said Anson, and the image of the bird changed to that of a large heavily-toothed lizard.

"Nine planes," said Hodge. "What is that?"

"Is that a Tyrannosaurus Rex?" I asked.

"The intel didn't give it a name, but it's a close match. About twice the size, though."

"We'll be out in the dark with that?"

"The intel says they sleep at night. Too cold for them to move around."

"Nine planes," Hodge said again.

"Just walk fast," said Cassidy.

Hodge smirked. "Need be, I'll run the whole way."

~*~

To avoid detection, Anson flew low and slow, skimming the top of the canopy. This was going to be a tight caper with a high reward—in and out.

During the long afternoon trip, we each fell into our ritual. Hodge polished up Lucinda and then wiped her with a dark powder to dull any shine he may pick up in the night. I mentioned to him that Lucida was a bit overkill. "Nine planes," was all he said.

Cassidy was on the bridge with Anson, and Rhia and Rhoe spent the journey playing dice for favors with Bailer. Their laughter soothed the tension.

And me—I wasn't taking any chances. I went over the intel and the holo-map.

With their acrobatic stealth, the twins could easily do the job alone, and on another planet. That's the way it would have gone. But I didn't know what to expect in that jungle in between the Jentu and the compound. Hodge was a bit brute force for the infiltration, but I thought that may come in handy along the way. So, I decided there would be four of us. Hodge and I would escort Rhia and Rhoe. They'd go in first—to disable security—and then we would assist with the target.

When the ship set down, we gathered in the galley. I could tell the crew was tense. It had nothing to do with the job. It had everything to do with Will.

"I know you're all thinking it," I said. "How'd they catch up with us? Well, we've had a pretty good run for the past hundred cycles, sticking mostly to free ports and open colonies. But it was bound to happen."

"Yeah," said Hodge. "But that fella recognized us. He pointed right to you."

"Do you think that Bureau Boy, Stetson, went back on his word?" asked Anson.

Cassidy answered for me. "No," she said. "He was from the old school. He may have been dirty, but he's a man of his word. If he said he'd scramble the wire, then that's what he did."

That riled Hodge. "A human's word means nothing to me," he said. "You told him we'd be back if our faces popped up on any of the Bureau detection systems." Hodge stood up. "I say that as soon as we finish up here, we plot a course back to the Argentine moons."

"It wasn't him," said Cassidy.

"I agree," I said. "Will told me he knew his contact—from before. The guy just turned on him."

"As soon as we finish, we have to go back for Will," Cassidy said.

"You think he's still alive?" Rhia asked.

Cassidy bit into her lower lip, and then said, "I don't know. He knows how to blend as well as us."

"His middle parted with him on the flight deck," Hodge said.

Cassidy snapped back, "But do you know he's dead?"

Hodge's brow went up with alarm. "Well no," he said. "None of us do for sure. But he took a—"

"Exactly," Cassidy said harshly. "We don't know for sure."

"Well, don't yell at me. I didn't leave him. The Captain did."

Five sets of blue eyes went to mine. "We know for sure. Cassidy. You saw his face. He was there and then he was gone. That's how he got left in the first place. There was no one to pull out."

"But we have words together. We have a protocol."

Cassidy was right. We did have words, and if we let those slip then our bond would wear thin.

"It's true," I said. "You all know it. We have words and the protocol is that when the field is hot, no one on the team, dead or alive, gets left behind. We'll drop the load, collect our pay and then make the rendezvous. If Will's not there, we'll hit Teller again."

"Yeah, that sounds good," said Hodge. "I say we look for him, sure. But in the meantime, we'll be safer without him."

Rhia gave Hodge a puzzled glare. "What do you mean 'safer?'" she asked.

"Well, when I was working in the space station maintenance, I saw a wanted poster in the constabulary for eight mortal Syns."

"Your point?" Rhoe asked.

"Captain says the humans don't know what we look like, and without Will, there are only seven of us." Hodge held up his hands as if his point should have been obvious to all of them.

I grinned and watched the others throw pillows across the room at the child-minded Hodge. But the childlike gem wasn't lost on me. Hodge was right; our off-world kick murder squad was made up of something humans tended to embrace: seven deadly Syns.

~*~

The run felt good. I'm not going to lie about that. The sweet air, untainted by industrialization, was an exhilarating elixir, and with each breath I drank, I found more strength. It'd been too long since my feet had beaten firm ground, and years since I was planet side without a full battle suit squeezing me tight. That was no small thing. Unencumbered, my legs swiftly cut through the gravity, propelled me forward, instinctually pouncing from crag to rock. Hodge and the twins must've felt the same. At their tail, I watched as they glided down the valley's natural path. Bathed in starlight, their shadows licked the terrain behind them, a black liquid mercury darting into the dark of the canopy, emerging in the glades.

But as we approached the heart of the valley, the canopy swallowed the bright moonless sky, and our trek far beneath turned dark. It was in the darkness that the forest came alive—ruffling, cracking, rattling—a myriad of nocturnal beings in every direction. We continued at the same clip, our ocular augments guiding the way. The floor of the jungle stretched out, shaded in hues of deep green. Training and conditioning overtook any inclination to be distracted by the peripheral silhouettes and eyes. No matter the planet, the natural law was the same: *Keep moving and the creatures will part your way, stop and...* Well, we weren't about to stop.

The air was heavier, warmer, wetter, and pungent on the jungle floor. I immediately felt the weight on my lungs. But we didn't slow. Hodge was picking up the pace. The larger undergrowth in this part of the valley grew farther apart, widening the path between the thick trunks, clearing our way to the compound. The counter in the low corner of my eye told me we were only two klicks from the walls and closing fast. I was already planning the incursion when, from our left, a deafening thwack sounded out, followed by a thrum. We all stopped in our steps and aimed to the skyward direction of the noise. From the dark void above, there was nothing—and then the fast-approaching silhouette of a giant limb. The four of us jumped back, and the tree-sized branch crashed down, shaking the ground where we had stood. I could only describe what followed as the sound of thunder and a wave of rancid heat. Looking up from where the massive branch landed, my augments detailed the wide, gaping, heavily-toothed maw of a roaring beast, a creature as mighty as a tyrannosaurus rex, yet five times the size.

We had stumbled upon a sleeping giant.

Hodge brought the barrel end of Lucinda up toward a cavernous, screaming mouth.

I had to react, to stop Hodge from shooting. We were too close to the compound to let out fire. And we were too close to the beast to scream.

It took all of my focus to chin chip, "No! Don't fire!"

Hodge swung his head to me. Even in augment I could see the twisted look on his face—divining whether to listen to me or naught. But for the sake of our lives, he didn't fire.

The creature's long cry wound down. It near closed its razor-toothed jaws and then opened them again, chewing the air as it woke. More of the rancid odor of decomposition settled upon us, as whatever had been cast from that lizard's howl floated to the forest floor.

Rhia and Rhoe gazed at each other and then, in unison, stepped back into the side of the path, away from the beast, taking the lead. Hodge gave me the eye and I returned with a subtle nod. We, too, stepped back.

One, two, three slow steps. I thought we were slipping away, that the mammoth lizard had not detected us. But on the fourth step, the creature let loose another thunderous roar, this time darting its head in our direction.

I'm not sure if I chin chipped it first, or if our legs were already moving. But I yelled, "Run." And we did. Directly away from the beast and into the forest deep.

We didn't look back to see if the creature had taken chase. We didn't need to. The cracking and thwacking of the splintering forest was at our backs, as were the repeated screeching roars, and with every foul-odored roar, the heat of the lizard beast's breath tickled the flesh of my neck.

But as close as the monster trailed, we still stayed—if even by a meter—out of its reach.

Rhia and Rhoe moved with the least resistance—somersaulting and cartwheeling over branches Hodge and I could only dive or tumble over, but we all pressed on the same. We'd run a klick through the black—grasses grazing our cheeks, fallen branches and other unseen obstacles hindering our way—when we came to the bank of the river and the opening of the sky. The rushing waters foamed white in the starlight, too rough for us to cross. But Hodge, the furthest down river, didn't hesitate to shift direction to the shoreline into a full run. The twins and I followed his lead, expecting the beast to do so in turn.

But the giant lizard didn't follow.

Perhaps he was confused by the river's edge, or maybe it was the open night sky that held him at bay. Or maybe the creature was satisfied we had been chased from its domain. Because the monster stopped there, let off one final deafening roar, and then, if I were to guess by the echoed crackles and snaps, returned to heart of the valley.

Though we were diverted, we continued with our plan. We followed the river to the compound walls.

~*~

ABOUT THE AUTHORS

Philip Harris was born in England but now lives in Canada where he works for a large video game developer. Not content with creating imaginary worlds for a living, he spends his spare time indulging his love of writing. His published books include **The Girl in the City Trilogy** and an homage to the old pulp science fiction serials - **Glitch Mitchell** and the **Unseen Planet**.

His short fiction has appeared in numerous anthologies and magazines including **The Jurassic Chronicles, Bones, Uncommon Minds, The Anthology of European SF**, and **Peeping Tom**. He has also worked as security for Darth Vader.

For more information, visit
chrisp solitarymindset.com

Ernie Howard was born on January 29,1977 during a Minnesota blizzard. His two story telling parents almost didn't make it to the hospital in their beat up blue Cadillac. Ernie is the writer of **Write Something!**, a book about the illusion of Writers Block. *A World Without*, a Science Fiction book about the love between a husband and wife, and the darkness that can come into a marriage. *Walter*, A Science Fiction book about a boy who is an outcast who makes a friend with a man that speaks to him through his television. Ernie lives with his wife and 3 boys in Henderson, NV, where he dreams up new stories, and tries to live everyday to the fullest.

Paul K. Swardstrom is a husband and a father, a music teacher by day and family man at night. I write when I can and am enjoying the ride.
A Sun Devil who grew up all over but remembers Michigan fondly, I have settled in Oregon.

Daniel Arthur Smith is the author of the international bestsellers *Hugh Howey Lives*, *The Cathari Treasure*, *The Somali Deception*, and a few other novels and short stories. He also curates the phenomenal short fiction series *Tales from the Canyons of the Damned*.

He was raised in Michigan and graduated from Western Michigan University where he studied philosophy, with focus on cognitive science, meta-physics, and comparative religion. He began his career as a bartender, barista, poetry house proprietor, teacher, and then became a technologist and futurist for the Fortune 100 across the Americas and Europe.

Daniel has traveled to over 300 cities in 22 countries, residing in Los Angeles, Kalamazoo, Prague, Crete, and now writes in Manhattan where he lives with his wife and young sons.

For more information, visit danielarthursmith.com

~*~